Also, by Michael Palmer

The Last Green Flash

No Cappuccino in the Afternoon

Under the Marula Tree

A Collection of Short Stories

Michael Palmer

authorHOUSE®

AuthorHouse™
1663 Liberty Drive
Bloomington, IN 47403
www.authorhouse.com
Phone: 833-262-8899

Published by AuthorHouse 06/21/2024

ISBN: 979-8-8230-2700-7 (sc)
ISBN: 979-8-8230-2699-4 (e)

Library of Congress Control Number: 2024910495

Print information available on the last page.

Any people depicted in stock imagery provided by Getty Images are models, and such images are being used for illustrative purposes only. Certain stock imagery © Getty Images.

This book is printed on acid-free paper.

Dedication

This book is dedicated to our grandson, Henry James.
We hope your life will be full of many interesting and amazing stories.

And, of course, to Brittany and Sean for giving us a chance to
be a grandparent.

My love to all of you

Contents

In many cultures in Africa, the Marula Tree is known as the "marriage tree" as it is seen a symbol of fertility and is used in a cleansing ritual before marriage.

It is also known as the elephant tree that bears the fruit that "drives elephants mad."

Under The Marula Tree

"Over there, just to the right, about 50 yards. Do you see it?"

"Under the marula tree?" I asked.

"Yes, yes, that's the one."

The marula tree, I thought. With its straight trunk and distinct rounded crown. The tree that is only found here in the warm, frost-free regions of sub-equatorial Africa. A tree whose succulent fruit is enjoyed by many safari animals.

The old elephant was alone. Its wrinkled, creased, and crusted skin evidence of the inescapable African environment. Probably too slow to keep up with the herd.

"Do you see the spot, the crease of the ear. Aim for that spot."

The old elephant raised its huge tusks off the savanna grass. Lifting its trunk upwards into the marula tree in search of the succulent, yellow-skinned fruit.

"The elephants' favorite fruit," my hunting guide had told me. "According to Zulu folklore, elephants will eat the fermented fruit until they get drunk. The folklore became so widespread, that the nickname for the marula tree quickly became the elephant tree."

"That spot at the crease of the ear, will result in an instant kill. That spot leads directly to the brain."

Looking at the old elephant, I turned to my guide, "how old?"

"Elephants can live to be over 100 years old, but I would guess this one's around 80."

Interesting, I thought, sad too. The old elephant and I were the same age. But there was one big difference. I was the one holding the fifty-caliber rifle with its 500 grain solid bullets.

"Are you going to take the shot? This is the last day of your hunting safari. You don't want to go home empty handed."

Yes, this was the last day of my personalized hunting safari. Hunting elephants in the South African brush. For the past three days, from sunup until sunset, bouncing over the harsh African terrain, in an old Jeep, in search of the perfect "tusker." That one gigantic tusker, the world's largest land mammal, guaranteed to provide me with "the hunting experience of a lifetime."

It was late June; the wet season was over. Everything was so green; wildflowers were in bloom. The marula tree was bursting with ripened fruit. But the old elephant looked tired. Age was catching up to him. He didn't even look that interested in the tree's fruit. Perhaps he was only there for the shade?

"Too late, you waited too long."

The old elephant turned his back to us. He wasn't ready just yet.

"Is he male or female?" I asked.

"Definitely a male."

"How can you tell?"

"The size. Males are larger. And males have a larger and more rounded forehead."

"How come he's alone?"

"Because his job is done."

"Job? What job?"

"The older male elephant is a mentor to the young males in the herd. The older males teach the younger males how to navigate the terrain, where to find water, food, actually how to survive."

"Seems important. So why don't they stay with the herd?"

"Well, the herd is female dominated. Once the young males have acquired important survival skills, their mentors are no longer needed, or welcomed."

"So, they leave?"

"Well, wouldn't you? No longer needed."

I didn't answer. But I understood. Suddenly, I understood how the old elephant felt. Alone, under the marula tree. No longer needed.

"Welcome to corporate America," my younger sister said. Of course, she had tenure at a major university.

As for me. For 40 years with the company, I watched younger employees join the firm. Like the old male elephant, I mentored the young employees. Training them in the skills they would need to succeed. Training them to one day replace me. I wasn't ready to leave, to retire, but I had become redundant. I was no longer needed. And so, like the old elephant, I was told to leave.

The old elephant turned. He was facing us. Could he see me, I wondered? Did he know we were both no longer needed?

"A straight head shot is very difficult. You should wait for him to turn."

But he didn't turn. He just looked at us. Could he even see, I wondered? Perhaps his eyesight, like mine was fading. Macular degeneration, my optometrist said. Nothing we can do.

"Does he ever rejoin the herd?" I asked

"No, never. But sometimes they'll bond with other older males. But no, they're not welcomed back to their original herd."

"Jesus, that's so sad," I replied.

"Yes, and that's why we only hunt the old bull elephants. They are no longer wanted, no longer useful."

"So, we're putting him out of his misery."

"I guess that's one way of looking at it."

It certainly is, I thought. Out of his misery. I too wanted out of my misery. Shortly after I was let go, no longer needed, I thought about it. That night I held the full bottle of sleeping pills in my hand, thinking why not. Like the old elephant. End it now.

But I didn't. Wrote a check for $60,000 to hunt old elephants instead. Jesus, what was I thinking? Shooting old elephants!

The old elephant slowly turned. He was sideways now. His big ear was flopping back and forth. The crease where the ear started was waiting for me.

"Now, shoot now."

I raised the rifle and took aim. Through the scope I saw the crease. I also saw the eye of the elephant. He was looking at me. He knew what was coming. He looked like he was ready. His last offering would be for me to have the "hunting experience of a lifetime." Yes, that would give his life meaning. A trophy for me. Stories to tell my friends. How I brought down a majestic tusker.

I turned to my guide. He was waiting for me to shoot.

"Did my check clear?" I asked.

"What?"

"My check for this hunt. My check to put this old elephant out of his misery?"

"Yes, of course it did."

"Good," I said, as I pulled the trigger.

The old elephant was startled. He let out a roar. So loud I thought. So majestic.

The bullet logged in the trunk of the marula tree. The force was so great that the fruit rained down like a fierce storm in the African rain season.

The old elephant was almost out of sight now, but he turned and looked back. He was confused. Just like my guide.

I stood up and started walking towards the marula tree.

"What the hell was that all about?" He asked.

"That, oh, that. I just wanted to try the fruit from the marula tree."

"What?"

"Come on join me. Let's get drunk."

A Summer in Sicily
with Alexander

"Buongiorno," Giovanni exclaimed, as I entered his La Dolce Vita Cafe.

"Buongiorno," I replied, convinced that my pronunciation wasn't even close to his.

But at least I understood what Giovanni was saying. Buongiorno, good morning. And I suspect he appreciated my attempted greeting. At least, I hoped so.

I had settled into my rental apartment in a small village on a mountain top overlooking the Ionian Sea.

Off in the distance, the toe of Italy, although in my mind it was more like the toenail of Italy. The southernmost tip of the Italian Peninsula. Yes, to me it was more like a giant toenail entering the Ionian Sea.

I was in Sicily, in Forza d'Angiò in the province of Messina.

It was the summer, and it was hot. Like a blast furnace, the travel agent warned.

But I wasn't going to Sicily for the weather, and I figured high in the mountains, how hot could it be? Surely there would be cool Mediterranean breezes.

"Why Sicily?" she asked.

I didn't answer and she didn't ask again.

"Coss ti piacerebbe," Giovanni asked.

What do I want, I thought. I've been coming here every morning for two weeks and he still asks me what I want.

"Cappuccino, per favore," I replied

"Si," he said with a big smile.

Just then Alexander walked into the cafe.

We had met shortly after I arrived.

He was a big guy. Big all over.

When I first saw him, I thought way too many morning croissants with that morning cappuccino.

"Buongiorno, Alexander. How are you, I mean, come stai?"

"Bene, molto bene … Michael … Michael Corelone," he said with a wink and a chuckle.

Michael Corelone. Thanks to Alexander, that had become my nickname, and why not since Francis Ford Coppola's 1971 Godfather film was shot here. At least some of the scenes, like the wedding of Michael and Apollonia. The church, the Cathedral of Santa Maria SS Annunziata was within shouting distance of the cafe.

Actually, almost everything in Forza d'Angiò was within shouting distance of the cafe. With a population of 835, it was easy to see why.

With his cappuccino and pistacchio filled croissant in hand, Alexander settled into the chair across from me.

"So, Alexander, any plans for today?" I asked stirring the foam into my cappuccino.

"You do know, you're not supposed to do that?" was his answer.

"Huh?"

"Cappuccino should not be stirred."

"But why?"

"You're disturbing the balance."

"The balance?"

"Yes, you want each sip to have the right amount of balance between the coffee and the steamed milk. But now you've disturbed the balance and it will not taste the same."

"Oh?"

"And stirring cappuccino ruins the aesthetic, gives it a muddy appearance."

"But why did I get a spoon with my order."

"It's for a tourist."

"If they want sugar?"

"If they must, but properly steamed milk is naturally sweet, so why add sugar?"

"My gosh, Alexander, I didn't realize there were all these rules to drinking cappuccino."

"Well, if you think there are a lot of rules here in Forza d'Angiò, order a cappuccino in Milan."

"Really?"

"Well, the cup must arrive resting on a saucer with the handle facing right and a small spoon on the same side. If sugar is added, it must be mixed from top to bottom, never clockwise or counterclockwise. The spoon must never be licked and never used to collect the foam from the bottom of the cup, and chocolate sprinkles should never …"

"Okay, Alexander, you've made your point, now let's enjoy our cappuccino.

"Si."

As I lifted my cup, I noticed a slight smile and a nod of approval from Alexander.

"I'm glad to see you're drinking your cappuccino the correct way," he said.

"What?"

"The little finger on your hand holding the cup."

"What about it?"

"It's never extended."

"I guess that's for drinking tea," I replied with a chuckle, "like in England."

"Perhaps, but this is Italy. We don't drink tea here. Only coffee. The drink that Italy introduced to the world."

"Not true, Alexander, that's not true."

"Sure, it is."

"Sorry, Alexander but Ethiopia is considered to be where coffee came from when in 800 AD a goat-herder named Kaldi introduced the drink."

Alexander frowned, shook his head slightly side to side and mouthed the words no way.

And so that's how it went for the next two months. Morning lessons from Alexander on Italy, actually how to live as an Italian, how to be an Italian.

So, for example, I was schooled in how to eat pizza - you cut it with a knife and eat it with your fork; what time to switch from ordering cappuccino to espresso - preferably 11:00, but certainly no later than noon; not to order a latte - unless you want a glass of milk; never ask for butter for your bread; never ask an Italian if they have a relative or a friend who's in the mafia; never put cheese on fish; never open an umbrella indoors; never gift someone a wallet without money inside; never give an uneven number of flowers - unless they are grieving over the death of someone.

And then there were the hand signals.

Every time I asked Alexander if I could teach him something American, he would decline.

"Why do I need to know," he would say, "we're not in America, we're in Italy."

And so, I stopped asking and he continued teaching.

Now at 39,000 feet flying across the Atlantic Ocean at the end of my holiday, I realize that introducing Alexander to American culture, whatever that is, would add no value to his idyllic life at 2,600 feet overlooking the Ionian Sea and the tip of Italy from his small village of Forza d'Angiò.

Perhaps next summer Michael Corleone will return to Forza d'Angiò and to the La Dolce Vita Cafe. Perhaps then Alexander can convince me that coffee was first introduced to the world in Italy.

Perhaps!

Sandy Koufax and Roy Campanella

I was in the backyard. Throwing rocks. I loved to throw rocks. At anything, but mainly at trees. The further the tree the better.

I thought I was Sandy Koufax. The Brooklyn Dodgers best pitcher. Yes, I was Sandy, every morning with those rocks. Roy Campanella was my catcher, too. "Strike three," I shouted, "you're out," as the rock hit its mark.

Jeffery and Jessica were there too. Mom let them out in the morning to be with me. Jeffery was my German Shepard and Jessica was my sister's beagle. I thought of them as my outfielders.

Jeffrey played right field. Jessica was faster, so she was my center fielder. Jeffrey was bigger. I considered him my linebacker during the football season. Jessica was way too small for football, so she would sit out that season until spring training. She was a girl too. So, football was really out of the question for her.

"Ball four, take your base." Jesus, I missed that tree four times in a row. Not one strike. What's wrong Sandy? Get it together, we're in a tight race for the pennant with the Giants.

The Giants. The New York Giants. Fans in the Bronx loved the Giants, but not those in Brooklyn. Giant fans use to call us the bums, Brooklyn bums. It just made us want to beat them all the more.

Willie Mays was the next batter. "Better play deep," I shouted to my outfielders. "This guy can hit."

Jeffrey and Jessica were not impressed. They certainly weren't worried about Willie. They were chasing a rabbit near the garden.

"I guess I'll have to strike you out, Willie." I was shouting at the tall maple tree about 30 yards to my left.

Brooklyn versus New York. It was always intense. At first, I didn't know who to root for. After all, my mom was born in Brooklyn and my dad was from the Bronx. Difficult decision. Uncle Joe told me I should have rooted for the Yankees.

"I can't do that, Uncle Joe, they're in the American League."

"And that's where they play real baseball," he would always reply.

One night he took me to a game at Yankee Stadium. The Yankees won, and they hit three home runs in one inning."

On the ride home, Uncle Joe said, "Now that was baseball. Real baseball."

Neglecting to mention the fact that he was born in Queens, I simply said, "it was okay."

Striking out Willie Mays on three straight pitches, I thought to myself, now that's baseball, real baseball. Screw the American League.

My imaginary team was always in the field. I still hadn't figured out how we could hit, but that was okay, because I liked throwing rocks. Someday, maybe, I would be throwing baseballs, not rocks.

I did have a baseball once. Well, it really wasn't mine. My dad went to a baseball game at the Polo Grounds. The Giants were playing the Cubs. My dad came home with a baseball. It was signed by Willie Mays.

He put the baseball on the fireplace mantle. It was his pride and joy. He would show it to everyone who came to the house. "Look, look at who signed this. Willie Mays."

But Jimmy wanted to play catch. I don't have a ball, I told him. "What about that one, up there, he said, pointing to the fireplace.

"Oh, come on," Jimmy pleaded, pounding his catcher's mitt. "You can pitch."

How could I turn that down? My chance to be Sandy Koufax with a real baseball. Jimmy would be Roy Campanella.

Smack! The ball hit Jimmy's glove. "Faster he shouted, let's see what you've got."

"Ok," I took a deep windup. Just like Sandy. And let it fly.

The ball sailed over Jimmy's head. A good five feet over his outstretched catcher's mitt. It hit the ground, and rolled through the muddy dirt, before stopping just before the pond.

We both ran to retrieve it. "Lucky it didn't go in the water," Jimmy said.

Picking up my dad's baseball, I noticed the mud. The ball was caked in mud. "Oh, shit, I'm in trouble now."

"Just rub it off, it will be fine." Jimmy offered.

I was skeptical, but then what else could I do.

"Perhaps a little water would help too." Jimmy was pointing at the pond, just a few feet from where he had dropped his catcher's mitt.

Only a few drops, I thought. That should clean it up.

I rubbed. The baseball was actually coming clean. It would be okay.

As the mud fell from the baseball, I chuckled. Sandy didn't have to clean his baseballs. The umpire behind home plate made sure they were clean. The he would give to ball to Roy who would throw it to me. Yes, that's what the Brooklyn Dodgers did.

I kept rubbing.

The Yankees, I thought. Now they probably play with dirty baseballs, but not my Dodgers, and certainly not Sandy.

Rubbing, rubbing, rubbing. It was all off now. The mud was gone.

Holding up the baseball, my joy turned to panic. Not only was the mud gone, but so was the signature. "What happened to Willie Mays?" Jimmy said.

"Do you think he'll notice? Your dad, do you think he'll notice?"

We were both looking at the baseball on the mantle. "I hope not," was all I could say. "I hope not."

The next day, I was back on the field with Jeffery and Jessica.

Eddie Stanky was the batter. The shortstop. Always a tough out,

I thought. And of course, my outfielders would be no help. They had returned to the house.

Okay Eddie, it's just you and me and Roy. The first rock missed the tree. Ball one. The second was right one. "Strike one," I shouted at the top of my lungs.

Then he shouted. My dad shouted. "Michael, get in here right now. You've got some explaining to do."

Jesus, he finally noticed the baseball. Sandy Koufax was done for the day. Perhaps he'll be on injured reserve for a while. Oh well, he did strike out Willie Mays.

The Basement

"Built in the mid 1800s." the realtor said, "oldest house on the block. Of course, it's gone through many upgrades over the years."

"I'm not sure this is the right location for us."

"This is the most sought out location in town, and for you an easy walk to the university," she countered.

Yes, I could walk to work. She was right about that. Probably no more than 15 minutes. But still there was something unsettling about the house, especially the basement.

"Where does that door go?" I asked, pointing to a door at the far end of the basement.

"Not sure. Perhaps it was used for storage. Shall we look?"

"Not much light down here," I said as we worked our way through a maze of old boxes, brushing away the cobwebs. "Damp too."

"It's locked. I'll have to find the key."

Looking at the door, I could tell it hadn't been opened for a long time, many years I thought. Caked in decades of dust and dirt. Solid too, as I knocked on the dark wood.

"Not sure you'll find a key," I said. "I doubt if anyone has opened this door for years."

Climbing the old wooden steps up to the main floor, I felt it for the first time. It was like a cold breeze. Following me up those stairs, gently touching the back of my neck, and then I tripped, hitting my head on the steps in front of me."

"Are you okay," she asked.

"Yes, I must have missed a step."

The rest of the house was delightful. The main floor consisted of a large living room with a big fireplace, a kitchen, and a stately dining room with an old chandelier above the table.

"Does that stay with the house?" I asked pointing to the chandelier.

"But, of course, as well as the mirror over the fireplace. Did you notice the mirror?"

Turning towards the fireplace, I replied, "No, I didn't. Not sure how I missed it. It's enormous, all the way to the ceiling."

I looked at the old, cloudy mirror. I didn't want to tell her what I did see. It was very faint, but I could make out an image. An old man, in a red plaid shirt, with a white beard smiling at me. No, it couldn't be. Rubbing my eyes, I looked at the mirror again. Nothing this time. The image was gone. I must have hit my head harder than I thought.

The second floor of the old home was very bright and cheery. Three bedrooms and a large bathroom.

"I could convert one of these into my office," I said.

"Yes, that would work," my wife said from the large back bedroom, "but not this one."

Stepping into the back bedroom, I could see why. "What a view," she said, "this must be our bedroom. It just must."

The view of the mountains was breathtaking. "Yes, I agree, this will be our room." And then for the second time, I felt it.

"Did you feel that cold breeze?" I asked.

"No, but I suspect it's a little drafty in this old house. Perhaps that's what you felt."

"Yes, that's probably it," I replied, but not really convinced of what I had just said. It was like the basement stairs, that cold breeze, I thought to myself. Just then I noticed the hairs on my arm. They were standing straight up. My arms tingled. Had they too felt the cold breeze?

"We should do it, we should buy it," she said.

My God, she was in love with this place. How could I say no?

"But you haven't even seen the rest of the house."

"What's to see? The basement? I'm not interested in the basement. Nothing down there for me."

One month later we were moving out of our rented apartment into our house. I couldn't talk her out of it, but then I really didn't try that hard. Perhaps I was too curious to talk her out of it. Perhaps I needed to know.

Carrying a large box from the rented truck to the front door, I heard a voice behind me. "Need help with that?"

Setting the box down, I reached out to shake his hand. "Hi. Yes, I could sure use some help. My wife's at work today. She couldn't get the day off."

"Glad to help. I'm Joseph, by the way. But you can call me Joe"

"I'm Justin." I said. "Do you live around here?"

Joe smiled, then I noticed it. "That's quite a beard you have there, Joe."

"Yes, it is. Some people say I look just like Santa, it's so long and so white."

"So?"

"So what?"

"Do you live around here?"

"Oh, I used to, but that was a long time ago."

"Where do you live now?"

Joe waved his hand, "Oh, here and there."

"Any kids, Joe?"

"No, just Martha and me." I thought I saw a look of despair on his face, but then he smiled. "I guess the family line ends with me." Then another look of despair.

"And your wife, what does she do?"

"Oh, Martha, she passed in 1941."

"I'm sorry Joe."

"No, no it's okay. We had many good years together. Many."

Reaching down to pick up the box, Joe pushed my hand away. "Let me get that."

"Thanks, Joe. Just put it in the front room."

"The one with the fireplace?"

"Why, yes, that one,"

"Is the big mirror still there?"

"Yes, it is." Now I was really confused. How did he know about the fireplace, the mirror?

"Have you been in this house before?"

Joe just smiled. He doesn't want to answer I thought. Why?

"Hey Joe, I didn't catch your last name?"

"Barton. Just like the name of this town. Joseph Barton."

Setting the box in front of the fireplace, Joe looked at the mirror.

"Oh my God, I sure do need a trim. This beard is looking mighty shabby."

He smiled. I didn't know what to say, so I didn't say anything.

"Have you seen the basement?" he asked.

"Not yet." Could he tell I was lying?

"Well, I better get going. My wife's expecting me. It's our anniversary. I must get some roses, red roses. Those are her favorites."

"I'm confused Joe, I thought you said your wife died."

"Did I say that. Oh God, I'm sorry. I must be confused too. Anyway, glad I could help. Enjoy the house."

The house. The house. It's our house. My house. Why didn't he say your house? And what was that about his wife. First dead, then alive.

Walking out, Joe turned. "Check out the basement. Every house in Barton has a basement. Gives a house character."

I waved goodbye. I didn't say goodbye. I was too focused on Joe. "What the hell was that all about?" I thought.

Returning to the house, I immediately went to the phone.

"Tyler Realty, how can we help you?"

"Is Mrs. Crosby there?"

"Yes, let me patch you through."

"Hello, this is Mrs. Crosby."

"June, this is Justin. We're just moving in. Today."

"Oh, that's nice. Is everything going well?"

"I think so, but I just had a strange visitor. Said he once lived in the neighborhood. Very odd guy. Named Joe, Joseph Barton. Looked like Santa Claus too."

Then I heard the gasp.

"June are you okay?"

"He's back."

"Back, who's back?"

"Oh God, I thought that was finished."

"Finished, back? What are you talking about?"

"Joseph Barton, of course. Jesus, he's back."

Before I could continue the conversation, she hung up. I called back, but no one answered.

Try to remember. What did Joe say? Something about the basement. Gives a house character.

Opening the door leading to the basement, I wondered, should I really go down there? I reached for the light switch at the top of the stairs. Damn, the light must be out.

Easing myself down the stairs in the dark I reached the basement. My fingers fumbled for the light switch. Nothing. Jesus, the lights are out down here too. Perhaps it's a fuse, I thought.

Then I saw it. A sliver of light at the far end of the basement. Walking towards the light in the dark basement, I suddenly hesitated. My God, that light is coming from under the locked door.

Closer and closer. Standing in front of the locked door, I thought I heard laugher.

Reaching for the door handle, I realized the door was no longer locked. Slowly, ever so slowly I opened the door. Dust and dirt fell to the floor. The door creaked. The light inside grew more intense. The door was wide open now. My heart was racing.

At first, they didn't see me. Sitting across from one another at a table in the middle of the room. Roses, red roses on the table. They were holding hands. The man with his long white beard reminded me of ... or was it him? Then I noticed that red plaid shirt. He looked at me and smiled. Jesus Christ it was Joe. As he waved at me, the woman turned. I wonder, could it be? Could that be Martha?

I closed the door. The light from under the door suddenly went out. I was in darkness now. The laughing had stopped. I reached for the door handle. It was locked. It was locked again.

A few weeks later, my wife and I stopped at the town overlook. There in the tall grass, almost hidden from sight, I saw a commemorative plaque. I bent down to read it.

THE TOWN OF BARTON

HERE ON THIS HILL, THE FIRST SETTLERS LOOKED DOWN INTO THE VALLEY BELOW. WEARY FROM THEIR LONG JOURNEY, THEY DECIDED THEY WOULD SETTLE HERE. ONE HUNDRED OF THEM, FROM THE STATE OF MARYLAND. THE GROUP LED BY JOSEPH BARTON AND HIS YOUNG BRIDE MARTHA. JUNE 1, 1825

My wife came over to where I was standing. "I really love this town. And our new house, I can hardly wait to have guests."

I smiled. "Yes, that will be nice." I wanted to tell her we already had guests but thought that could wait for another day.

The Alarm Clock Radio

It was barely noticeable at the back of the top shelf.

I rose up on my tiptoes to get a better look.

Whatever it was, years of dust had provided a protective covering. Sheltering its secret.

How long had it been there, I wondered as I moved my hand towards the object.

Brushing the thick layer of dust aside, I coughed violently.

"Are you okay?" It was the shop owner.

"Yes, just the dust," I replied. "I'm fine."

I looked over at him.

Probably in his 80s, late 80s, I thought. Winter white hair, blood-flecked eyes, and a face chiseled by the passage of time. A slight tremble in his hand and a voice so soft that I struggled to hear.

But that was not all.

He had a captivating smile that quickly became the focus of my attention. Even the missing front tooth could not spoil his smile or turn me away.

"Would you like a glass of water?" He was staring up at me.

"No thanks, but I could use a rag to wipe the dust off this."

"Sure, give me a minute."

He shuffled away, favoring one leg. Osteoporosis, I thought. And too proud to use a cane.

He returned with a dirty rag.

"Sorry, but this is all I could find. Everything's dusty in here. Place hasn't been properly cleaned in years."

More like decades I thought.

"That's okay, it'll be fine." I said not wanting to embarrass the old man. But I could tell he was. I could see it in his face and in his eyes. His smile retreated. He looked much older now.

I cleared my throat and reached for his shoulder.

"Really, it's fine," I said again trying to be more convincing this time. "Thank you."

His smile reappeared and he handed me the dusty rag.

"You better stand back, there's likely to be a lot of dust."

"Probably there since the 30s."

"Excuse me."

"1931. That's when my dad opened this shop. In the middle of the depression."

"Jesus. During the depression."

"Yeah. He figured people were desperate to sell things. Needed money you know."

"Probably were."

"So, he travelled around in his beat-up truck and bought every antique he could lay his hands on."

I glanced over at the store front window. Although it was reverse, I could read it. John Dunn Antiques. And in small letters underneath, Established 1932.

"And you," I asked.

"John Jr."

"So, antiques are probably in your DNA."

"Been in this shop since the day I was born. Probably die in here too." His smile widened and he let out a soft chuckle.

I decided to extend his remarks hoping to prolong the humor.

"They'll probably have trouble locating your body under all the dust," I said.

I laughed, expecting the old man to join me. But he didn't. Then I noticed the sadness in his eyes. Clearly, I had hit a sensitive point with him.

"Did you like working with your dad?" I asked trying to break the tension I had created.

"Most of the time."

The object was free of dust now. I could see what it was. An old alarm clock radio.

I pulled if from the back of the shelf and held it out in front of me.

"I wonder how old this is?" I asked.

"Not sure," the old man said. His appearance suddenly turned very serious.

"Does it still work?"

"Suspect so."

"Can we try it?"

"Oh no, not this radio. Not in here."

"Why not," I replied turning the radio upside down.

"Because …"

"Jesus, look, it has vacuum tubes. Vacuum tubes. It must be really old."

The old man stayed silent for a long time. I could tell he was thinking about what he wanted to say.

Finally, he spoke.

"I remember the day my dad brought that radio to the shop. It was a day that changed his life."

"For the better."

"Yes, at first, but then …"

His voice trailed off. I felt he did so intentionally.

"How much?" I asked. "How much for this alarm clock radio?"

"It's not for sale. Sorry, I should have thrown that damn thing away a long time ago. I guess I forgot it was there."

"But I really want to buy it."

"No, it's not for sale."

"But why?"

The old man suddenly stepped back. Fear, I thought, he's afraid of something. The clock radio. He's afraid of the clock radio.

"It's… it's … cursed. That clock radio is cursed." He was almost shouting now. "The damn clock radio is cursed."

Then he fell silent. Perhaps second questing as to why he had begun to reveal some awful secret.

"How is that even possible?" I shot back. "How could a clock radio be cursed?"

Tired from standing the old man eased himself onto one of the antique couches.

"Don't know why. Just know it is."

Not accepting that for an answer I pressed on.

"Well how is it a curse?"

The old man sighed, he looked like he was ready to tell someone at last. To ease the burden of the mystery, the curse, which he had known for such a long time.

"You'll probably think I'm crazy," he said. "Completely off my rocker."

He sighed again and took a deep breath. Then he continued.

"But what I'm about to tell you is the truth."

"Okay." I said as I lowered myself in an easy chair directly in front of him. The mysterious radio was resting in my hands.

"That clock radio …" he paused. His glance fell to his hands which were trembling at a faster pace now.

"That clock radio not only tells your future, but it determines your future. And once determined, you can't change it. Good or bad, your future for that day, but that day only, is set in stone by this cursed machine."

"I don't understand."

"If you set the alarm for the next morning, whatever music or song you wake up to determines your fate for that day. You have absolutely no control over it, you are completely at the mercy of the alarm clock's song."

This is nuts, I thought. Yes, he is crazy.

"I can tell by the look on your face that you don't believe me. I guess I wouldn't if you were telling the story. But damn it, it's true. Every word is true. The curse is real."

"Assuming it is, I would still like to buy it."

"Why. Why would you want to buy it after what I just told you."

"I think it's a beautiful piece of work. It would look wonderful in my bedroom."

"But didn't you hear what I told you. This damn thing will take control of your life, your future. And once it does, there's no turning back."

The old man could see that I was determined to buy the alarm clock radio. He finally gave in to me and shrugged his shoulders.

"Okay it's yours, take it, I don't want anything for it, not even a penny."

"Well thanks."

"Don't thank me, and don't bring that damn thing back. I don't ever want to see it again."

Leaving the shop, I turned to look back at the old man. His head was in his hands, and his shoulders were slowly trembling. He looked like he might be crying, but I wasn't sure, and I wasn't about to go back to find out.

Walking the short distance back to my apartment I noticed that dark clouds were forming over the city.

As I reached the entrance to the building, the doorman quickly opened the door.

"Thank you, Mike," I said as I entered.

"You're welcome, Mister Jones."

"Looks like a bad storm is moving in."

"A big one I think by the looks of those dark clouds."

The elevator door opened, and I stepped inside. I was alone. Pushing the button to floor 5, I looked at the alarm clock.

"Naw, it can't be true. It can't be cursed. That's ridiculous," I said out loud, but also confident that Mike couldn't hear me.

Fifth floor, apartment 505. I was back home.

Setting the clock radio on the side table next to my bed, I plugged its cord into the electrical outlet.

As the clock face came to life, strange noises from inside the radio followed. Popping, cracking noises.

Probably from the dust, I thought. Just noises from the leftover dust heating up.

It was past midnight when I decided to call it a day. After all, it was now Monday, and I would be off to work in the morning. I decided to set the alarm. 6:30.

Just then I saw a flash of lightening out the window. Then thunder. And then the rain started. A torrential downpour began.

This is going to be a real mess in the morning, I thought. Especially since I walk to work. Better get out the umbrella.

Throughout the night I was jarred awake by the loud clap of thunder and the pounding rain against my bedroom window.

Yes, a real mess in the morning, I said as I struggled to go back to sleep.

6:30. The alarm clock clicked, followed by soft strumming on a guitar. I immediately recognize the singer. George Harrison. It was the Beatles.

Here comes the sun ...

I looked out the window, it was still raining. Hard too.

So much for the curse, I laughed.

A quick shower, then coffee, and I was ready to head out to work

It was still raining, thunder too, so I grabbed my umbrella and raincoat and headed for the elevator.

Mike was in the lobby as usual.

"Good morning, Mister Jones."

"Morning Mike."

"I doubt if you'll need those today," Mike said with a big grin on his face.

"Excuse me."

"The umbrella and raincoat. Not much use for them today."

"But it's ..."

I stopped mid-sentence and glanced out the lobby window.

"No way," I muttered. "Just a few minutes ago it was ..."

"You can leave the umbrella and raincoat with me. I can put them in the storeroom." It was Mike again.

"Sure Mike, thanks."

Stepping outside, into the sunshine, I shook my head.

"Just a freak coincidence," I said as I looked at the fast-drying sidewalk. "That's all."

Walking to the local police department, where I worked, I replayed the morning's events over and over.

Could it be, the clock radio? No way. Just a coincidence.

But, all day at work, I struggled, trying to explain to myself what had happened.

The storm, the song, the sun. Was there a connection? Could it be possible?

That night I set the clock radio, again.

I could hardly sleep wondering what would happen in the morning.

But at 6:30, I awoke to ABBA. The Swedish pop group was singing one of their most popular songs of the 70s.

Money, money, money…

Money, money, I thought, if only. If only I had enough money.

If I did, I would quit my job.

I hated walking the streets every day, writing parking tickets. The parking ticket Czar with a pencil for a gun, that's what they called me at work. Of course, the people I wrote tickets for called me a lot worse.

Jesus, if only. If only I had enough money.

Off to work again, but it wasn't raining money. Damn clock radio. It was just a joke, I was sure.

As I passed the local smoke shop, I glanced at the display in the store window.

Mega Lottery. Tickets on sale here.

Why not, I thought. Just one.

As I entered, the heavy smell of cigar smoke greeted me along with a short older man behind the counter.

"How many tickets?" He asked.

"Just one," I replied as I coughed violently from the cigar smell.

"Not a smoker, huh?"

"No."

"Well good for you, those damn things will kill you."

"But …"

"Oh, why do I work here?"

"Yeah."

"Hoping I sell a winning ticket, so I can retire on the winning ticket commission before it kills me. Did you know the seller gets 10%."

He was holding the one ticket in his hand.

"Perhaps it's this one," he said with a smile on his face. "Yes, I think it just might be this one."

Out in the fresh air, with my one ticket, I headed off to work.

The day went by quickly although my boss was upset that I didn't write enough parking tickets.

"Jesus, Jones, are you slacking on the job? Hit that quota or else." He said as I was leaving.

"Or what?"

"Or you'll be out on your ass, that's what."

We never did get along, Chief Parker and me. From the day the city offered me the job, twenty years ago.

"I don't care for your type," he said on the first day.

"I guess you'll have to live with it," was my only reply.

And from that point on, it was all downhill. Insults, crappy schedules.

"Why do you stay on?" a friend asked.

"Probably to piss him off," I replied early on. "Besides, the exercise is good."

But of course, now, I hated the job and more, I hated Parker. In my darkest moments, I could imagine myself actually killing him.

That night I didn't set the alarm clock. After all, it was Friday, and I had the weekend off. Someone else would have to write those damn parking tickets.

Even without the alarm clock I was up early.

Leisurely breakfast at my favorite cafe and then I decided to take a walk.

Passing the smoke shop, I felt the urge to go in. Not sure why, as I didn't care much for the cigar smell.

But I did and there was the old man.

"Morning," he said without looking up. "How's your day going?"

"Okay."

I coughed and he looked up.

"Oh, it's you."

"Yes."

He was smiling, just like yesterday.

"What can I get you?"

"The morning paper, if you have one."

"Checking the numbers?"

"Huh?"

"From last night's mega lottery. The numbers. The ticket you purchased."

"Oh, I forgot all about that. Was it last night?"

"My god man, the largest jackpot in the history of the lottery. And you didn't bother to watch."

"No, I just forgot and after all there is no way I'm going to win."

"We'll, why don't we just check."

"Sure, if you say so."

I pulled the ticket from my wallet and put on my reading glasses.

"I'll read you the numbers," he said turning the pages of the newspaper.

"Okay."

"22."

"Got that."

"27."

"Got that too."

"13 and 40."

"Yes, I have both of those."

"2."

I said nothing. I just stared at the ticket. I was blinking trying to read the numbers.

"I said 2."

"Err, yes, I have 2." I was breathing fast now. My hand was shaking.

"Well just one more."

"Wait a second, I need to catch my breath."

I stepped back from the counter. As I did, I heard ABBA's song in my head.

Money, money, money…

"No need to tell me the last number," I said, bursting out in laughter.

"Really?"

"Yes, I'm sure I have it."

"But."

"It's 17."

The old man said nothing. I continued.

"So, it looks like you'll be retiring soon."

I slowly turned and walked out of the shop.

The clock radio, I thought. My god, it's real.

I rushed back to antique shop. John Jr. was there.

When he saw me, he held up his hands as if to ask me to stop approaching him.

"John, it's me …"

"I remember you, and the answer is no."

"What?"

"I'm not taking the alarm clock radio back."

"No, no, I don't want to return it. I just want to thank you."

"Oh."

"It brought me nothing but good fortune."

"But …"

"I'm so happy and I just wanted to share some of my good luck with you."

"No, please. I don't want anything to do with that evil device, nothing."

"But it's not. It's not cursed, it's not evil."

"You'll see. My dad thought the same thing. But it'll pull you in and then …"

"No, John, you're wrong. It's been a blessing."

"Blessing hell. I don't want anything to do with it."

"But …"

"Now please leave."

Returning to my apartment, I was confused. Why was John so upset? What did he mean by his dad thinking the same thing?

But that night I set the clock alarm.

John would see. He would see what a blessing this clock was. I would show him.

6:00 and the alarm went off. It was Elvis Presley this time, with one of his most famous and romantic songs.

For I can't help falling in love with you …

I chuckled.

Well, that's not about to happen. All my attempts at numerous dating sites had produced nothing. Not a bite. I was destined to live a single, boring life.

It was Sunday morning and like every Sunday morning for the last ten years I headed to the small cafe across the street for breakfast.

"Mister Jones, we've been expecting you. I saved a cinnamon roll for you."

"Thanks Tommy."

Tommy was the owner of the Morning Side Cafe. I had known him for ten years and still he insisted on called me Mister Jones.

"As you can see, we're pretty full this morning."

"Well, that's good for business, isn't it?"

"Yes, but I can't have my favorite customer stand and wait."

"No problem, Tommy. I can wait."

"I tell you what Mister Jones. My younger sister, Linda, is visiting and she's sitting alone at a table. Follow me."

"But Tommy …"

"No buts, Mister Jones, I'm sure she would like someone to talk to."

And talk we did. Linda and me. Over coffee and cinnamon rolls. For hours. Through lunch time.

She was single, alone, like me.

We talked about our past, about our hopes and dreams for the future. We laughed. A lot.

It was like we had known one another our whole lives.

And so, thanks to Tommy, our relationship began that day at the Morning Side Café.

Over the next month while Linda was in town, we saw one another every day.

It was the most wonderful month of my life. A month with Linda. So wonderful, that I even forgot the alarm clock. Didn't set it once.

And then Linda was getting ready to leave. Her vacation was over.

I drove her to the airport and walked her to the gate.

"Linda, I've had a wonderful month, thanks to you."

"Me too, Larry."

"I wish it didn't have to end."

She looked away like she was embarrassed. But I knew I had to tell her. I had to follow up with Elvis' song that I heard a month ago. I couldn't let this moment pass without telling her.

"Linda."

"Yes."

"I think I'm … falling in love with you."

There I said it and it felt good.

Linda looked down at the floor. I felt I had made her uncomfortable.

"I'm sorry Linda, I just had to tell you."

"I don't know what to say, Larry."

"That's okay."

"No, it's not. I didn't mean to lead you on."

"Oh."

"I thought we were just friends, nothing more. I'm sorry."

She turned and headed to the gate. She turned so quickly that she didn't see the tears forming in my eyes. I was glad she didn't see them. Now I was embarrassed.

How could I have misread her? I asked myself all the way home and even that evening when I was getting ready for bed. How could I have been so wrong.

Or was it the clock radio. Just leading me on. Fooling me into falling in love. Jesus, maybe John was right. It led me on and then … The damn clock radio.

Should I set alarm clock for the morning? Should I see?

The temptation was too great. It was set for 6.

6:00 and the click of the radio sounded. Then the voice of Frank Sinatra, old blue eyes,

And now the end is near ...

Jesus, I thought, as the song ended. What is that about? The end is near.

Dressing slowing, the lyrics continued to haunt me.

I wonder if I should stay in my apartment. Do I dare go out?

But it was Sunday morning, so I headed down to the lobby. There was Mike.

"Good morning, Mike."

"Morning Mister Jones. Heading over to Morning Side."

"Every Sunday. Cincinnati rolls and coffee."

"Like clockwork, Mister Jones."

"Yeah, I guess you could set your alarm to it."

As I exited the building, I thought about the radio alarm clock upstairs. Tonight, I'm throwing it out. I've had enough of it.

Stopping on the sidewalk, I started humming a tune. Across the street the neon sign in the window of the Morning Side Cafe was flashing open.

I stepped off the curb and on to the street. As I did, I saw Linda at the open door of the Morning Side Cafe. She was smiling and waving. She had returned. My first love was back.

I started running when I heard a shout behind me. It was Mike.

I turned. I couldn't hear him for all the traffic noise. But I did hear Frank Sinatra. Singing in my head.

I turned back to see Linda. She had her hands covering her mouth.

I turned back towards Mike and as I did, I saw it out of the corner of my eye.

Frank was singing

And now the end is near ...

Just as the speeding truck plowed into me.

31

Early Memories

When I close my eyes, I can still see it. Like it was yesterday.

1929 Fowler Avenue.

In New York City, The Bronx.

A small two-story home, with a single dormer on the roof for attic ventilation.

Built in 1915.

Living quarters on the first floor and bedrooms upstairs.

A downward sloping back yard with large trees.

A small workshop off the back of the home.

My memories are so vivid, beginning with my first.

I was 4 when my mother lifted me out of bed and carried me to the window. She opened the upstairs window overlooking the street below.

People were celebrating, horns were honking. The sounds were close and far away.

It was 7:03 in the evening, August 14, 1945. President Harry Truman had just announced that Japan had surrendered. World War II was officially over. It was V-J Day!

My mother was holding on to me. We were both at the open window. She was crying.

"Michael," she said, "try to remember this moment."

And I did, along with many more that followed at 1929 Fowler Avenue.

1929 Fowler Avenue. My grandfather, Michael Eugene Rizzo, lived there. My mother's father.

On June 2nd, 1888, Michael Eugene Rizzo and his father, Nicolas, arrived in New York on the ship, Cachemire. The two had departed from Naples, Italy. They were part of a growing number of Italian immigrants who had come to the United States in search of a better future.

Michael Rizzo was 12 years old.

The rest of the family soon followed.

Like many Italian immigrants they initially settled close to Little Italy in lower Manhattan.

Little Italy initially began to take shape when the first wave of Italian immigrants arrived in the 1840s. Like the influx of Irish immigrants escaping the potato famine in the 1840s, the masses of Italians arriving in America were fleeing hardships at home.

Italy continued to suffer into the late 1800s from droughts that destroyed the southern farmlands. With the Italian economy struggling, agricultural stagnation, and burdensome taxes, Italian men moved to America in an attempt to make and send money back to their families still living in Italy. Eventually, entire families located in America.

The biggest wave of Italian immigration began in the 1880s. Between 1880 and 1920, over four million Italians arrived in America, with tens of thousands settling in New York City alone. Many settled into an area of Five Points called "Mulberry Bend," which was part of the first "Little Italy" in New York.

The Five Points neighborhood in lower Manhattan got its name in 1881 because three streets – Orange, Anthony and Cross — intersected there, producing five corners, or "points." Streetcar signs could not fit all the street names, so they simply called it "Five Points."

Five Points was an overpopulated, disease, and crime-ridden area notorious for its tenement buildings and lawlessness. As the century neared its close, middle- and upper-class residents were fleeing the area, leaving only the poor, mostly immigrants, to suffer in its squalor.

It was also right around this time that Little Italy in Five Points reached its peak population. Almost 10,000 Italian-Americans lived in a roughly two square mile area.

Subsequently, many Italians who had immigrated, or were immigrating, to New York settled into other Italian enclaves, such as Little Italy in the Bronx; Bensonhurst and Bay Ridge in Brooklyn; and Staten Island.

1929 Fowler Avenue was approximately 15 miles from Little Italy in lower Manhattan and only 2 miles from Little Italy in the Bronx.

My grandfather was a widower. His wife, Amelia, died one week before I was born. She was 65.

I loved to watch my grandfather in his workshop. He would spend hours there, standing in front of his waist high wooden worktable. His tools hanging on the wall behind him.

I never knew what he was working on, but he looked happy and pleased.

On occasion I would run between the trees in the backyard, playing hide and seek with imaginary friends.

And in the evenings, in the bedroom, sometimes I would be joined by my older cousin, Buddy, who would tell me stories. Buddy also told me that one day he would fly jet planes for the Navy. Landing on and taking off from aircraft carriers. And he eventually did.

My grandfather loved to explore the outdoors. Perhaps it reminded him of his childhood in the hills of Calvello in southern Italy.

One day my grandfather came into the house carrying a handful of dandelion greens.

"What are you doing with those?" we asked.

"Cooking 'em," he replied.

And he did, and they were delicious,

And so it was, at 1929 Fowler Avenue.

The Eyes Have It

Richard was blind at birth.

That was forty-one years ago.

So, when his brother, Larry, told him the University Hospital called and asked if he might be interested in an experimental procedure, one that might restore his vision, he was excited.

He was so excited that he struggled to get the words out.

"What ... what did they say, Larry, tell me ... please tell me."

"Not much Richard, just that they suggested you come to the clinic."

"When ... when can I go."

"I have to call them back. Now, why don't you finish your breakfast, and then I'll call."

Richard was living with Larry ever since their parents went into a retirement home. Some in the family thought they moved early to get away from having to take care of Richard. When they did, the responsibility fell on Larry, their only other child.

Usually a slow eater, Richard finished his breakfast in record time. Gulping down the last of his coffee, he blurted out,

"Okay, okay ... call them. Tell them I'm interested."

The meeting was set for next Wednesday. Larry would have to take off work to take Richard. But he didn't really mind doing so as his job as a city health inspector had grown tiresome.

"Larry, is it okay for you to miss work?" Richard seemed concerned. Perhaps he was worried that Larry might have to cancel his meeting at the clinic. Or perhaps he was questioning whether he really wanted to go, whether he was just apprehensive about this experimental procedure.

"Sure, it's okay. Anyway, let someone else inspect those damn restaurant kitchens. As for me, I'm sick of looking for rat shit."

"At least you can see it," Richard replied, pointing to his motionless eyes.

Larry didn't reply as a feeling of guilt washed over him. He sat there staring at his coffee.

Sensing the uncomfortable silence, Richard burst out in laughter.

"Actually, that's probably an advantage of being blind."

The eye clinic was on the fourth floor. Richard had been there many times, so he usually felt comfortable there. But not this time. No, this time he was worried, tense, afraid. Strange, he thought, why aren't I excited?

"Richard, the doctor will see you now." It was the clinic nurse, Cindi. But even her soothing voice didn't help. Richard felt his stomach tighten and his hands shaking. Then he felt Larry's hand holding his, helping him up and guiding him across the waiting room.

The next hour consisted of technical talk, most of which fell on Richard's disinterested ears. The conversation among the doctors almost put him asleep, but then he was suddenly brought back to the present.

"So, Richard, we all agree you would be a good candidate for this procedure." It was Doctor Clark, the lead doctor. His hand was on Richard's shoulder.

"Huh?"

"You're a candidate, Richard. They can do it." It was Larry; he was almost shouting. "They can do the procedure."

"Oh."

"Richard, are you okay? Is anything wrong?" It was Doctor Clark again.

"Err... yes, I'm fine. Thank you, Doctor Clark."

The weeks went by, slowly, but finally the day of the procedure was almost here. Tomorrow. Richard was instructed to check in to the University Hospital at 7 in the morning.

He didn't sleep much, perhaps not at all.

And then Larry was driving him to the hospital. It was a drive they had taken many times and by now he could anticipate every turn and stop before it actually happened.

"I wonder what it's going to look like," Richard said.

"What?"

"The drive, the streets, the road. I wonder what it will look like. I wonder if it will seem different when I can see it."

"Oh," was all Larry could offer. But then he didn't want to dash Richard's hopes by telling him that the doctors told him that there was only a 30 percent chance of the procedure restoring Richard's sight.

"Best we don't tell him," Larry said. Doctor Clark agreed.

The operating room was cold, and all Richard could hear was the humming of machines. All he could feel was the pressure cuff around his upper arm, tightening, then loosening, over and over. Tightening and loosening.

Suddenly he felt very tired and almost numb. It came on so quickly, that it frightened him. But then he heard Doctor Clark's voice and his concern eased.

"Richard, Doctor Clark here. We will be starting the procedure shortly, but for now just relax.

And relax he did, to the point where he didn't hear Doctor Clark say, "okay team, let's give this our best shot. We can only do this once."

Richard was struggling to wake up. How long have I been sleeping, he wondered, and where am I?

He could feel a heavy blanket covering him from his toes to his chest. It was warm too. The pressure cuff was still on his arm, tightening and loosening. And there was a hand holding his.

"Richard, how do you feel?"

It was Larry.

"Where ..." was all he could say. His dry, and slightly irritated throat blocked his full response.

"In the recovery room, Richard. You're in the recovery room."

Indeed, he was and as for his eyes, when he opened them, all he saw was darkness. Darkness, just like always.

Richard sat up reached for his eyes and that's when he felt the gauze. It circled his entire head and covered his eyes.

"Richard," it was Larry again. "Don't pull at the covering over your eyes."

"Oh."

"Yes, Doctor Clark will explain all of that. For now, just lie back."

After what seemed like hours, a hand touched Richard's arm.

"How are you feeling?" Doctor Clark asked.

"Tired," Richard replied.

"Well, everything went as expected, so we'll..."

"Does that mean I can see?"

"So, we'll have to wait a few weeks to check on the results."

"A few weeks?"

"Yes, in a few weeks, we can remove the gauze, and then ..."

"I'll be able to see?"

"That's what we'll find out at that time."

"There's no way to know ... to know now?" Richard asked, his speech cracking in disappointment.

"No, not now," was all Doctor Clark could offer. "We must wait."

"But ..."

"Come back in two weeks and we will remove the gauze. In the meantime, the one thing you must avoid is a sharp blow to the head. Be careful not to fall, as that could reverse what we are attempting to achieve."

"That's it?"

"And please do not remove the gauze."

"Anything else?"

"That should do it. See you in two weeks."

Back home, Richard settled into an easy chair in the living room. Larry could sense that something was wrong.

"Richard, is everything okay?"

"I don't know. Perhaps I'm just anxious about waiting."

"That's understandable, but you really don't have a choice, so try to relax."

The days moved by slowly, and after a week, Richard felt the need to do something. Sitting in the kitchen, waiting for Larry to come home after work, he had reached a breaking point.

So, he decided he would remove the gauze.

Larry wasn't home and wouldn't be for at least an hour, so Richard thought, what the hell, just a little peek, and then he would put the gauze back. What harm could come of that?

He removed the metal clip holding the gauze in place. The gauze loosened, and he reached for the end of it. Slowly he started to unravel the gauze but after a few turns around his head, he hesitated.

He recalled the words of his doctor. Please do not remove the gauze. Should he stop?

"Oh, what the hell, do it," he muttered.

And so, he did.

The gauze slowly fell to Richard's shoulders. As he brushed it off it fell to his feet.

At first Richard held his eyes closed as tight as he could, fearing what he would see, or actually not see, if he opened them.

But the time had come.

Slowly he tried to open his eyes, struggling at first as the lids were crusted together from the after-surgery medication.

But finally … his eyes opened.

At first all he could see were shadows, blurry shadows.

Gradually his vision came into focus.

Before him was the living room, the large sofa where he spent hours, listening to the radio and waiting for Larry to return from work.

Looking down at his feet, he saw the medicine-stained gauze on the kitchen floor.

Turning to his right was a closed door, perhaps to his room, or perhaps to the outside.

He rose from the chair he had been sitting on, unsteady at first, and glanced around the room which had been his dark "prison" as he called it. Now it was full of light. Alive with light. He started to cry.

He lowered himself back onto the kitchen chair, and wiped the tears from his eyes, from his cheeks, and chin.

And then he turned back to the door.

It must be to the outside, he thought, recalling that Larry told him he would never close his bedroom door. He wanted it open, so he could hear him if needed.

Yes, the door must be to the outside.

"Do I dare?" he muttered to himself. "Do I dare open that door?"

He had been outside many times, going for a walk with Larry mostly, but this would be different. He would see all those things he had only imagined. Trees, buildings, cars, even the sidewalk, the uneven sidewalk which he had stumbled on many times.

Finally, the temptation was too strong. He decided to venture out.

Just a few steps, he told himself. That should be fine. A few steps on the uneven sidewalk.

He was steady now as he quickly moved to the front door.

Don't hesitate, he told himself. Don't turn back.

He pulled at the door, but it wouldn't open.

"Of course," he shouted, "it's locked."

Fumbling with the never before seen lock, he finally heard a click.

"That must be it."

And it was. The door was now ready to be opened.

Richard took a deep breath, two actually, and slowly opened the door.

As their apartment was on the ground floor, Richard only had a few steps before he would actually be outside. All he had to do was open the main door.

He stood there, looking out through the big glass doors, afraid of what he would experience, but excited too.

More deep breaths, and then he did it. He opened the main door and stepped into a world that had only been described to him. His heart was racing.

The rush of the early evening air greeted him. It was cool, but pleasant. His welcome to the outside, he chuckled.

Tall buildings - Larry called them skyscrapers- were everywhere. He almost fell over backwards trying to see the top of them.

The street in front of the apartment was full of traffic, cars and buses. Now he knew why it was so noisy in the apartment when Larry opened the window.

And on the sidewalk, a crush of people, somehow avoiding one another in their hectic pace to get somewhere.

Richard wondered if he was really ready for this world. Was it too much to take in? Perhaps he should retreat to the comfort of the apartment.

But he didn't. Instead, he started walking.

Coming to a busy intersection, he stopped with the crowd, waiting for the light to change.

When it turned green, the crowd of pedestrians pushed forward; Richard felt he was caught in a fast moving stream of people.

Halfway across the street, he noticed it off to his left. He couldn't believe what his restored vision was showing him.

As he paused and stared, people continued to rush by.

But why didn't they notice, he thought. Why aren't they stopping to observe what he was seeing?

His eyes took it all in, but his mind couldn't comprehend what he was looking at. It was both beautiful and ominous looking.

Finally, he grabbed the arm of a passerby and asked,

"Please can you tell me what that is?"

"What?" Was the reply.

"Pointing to the sky, Richard said, "that?"

"Christ, buddy, get the hell out of this crosswalk before you get run over."

But Richard couldn't move. He was in a trance.

Soon cars were blasting their horns. One irate driver yelled, "hey asshole, get out of the street, you're holding up traffic."

Still Richard stood his ground.

Suddenly a hand grabbed his arm. He turned. It was Larry.

43

"Jesus, Richard, let's get to the curb."

Safely on the sidewalk, Larry grabbed Richard by his shoulders.

"What were you thinking, Richard?"

"But ..."

"But what, Richard?"

"But didn't you see it?"

"What?"

"Those colors, those colors in the sky."

"Jesus, Richard, it was only a sunset."

"And nobody was looking at it. Nobody."

"Huh?"

"I don't understand," Richard said shaking his head.

"What?"

"Larry, what if you went blind right now? What would you want your last vision to be? The broken sidewalk beneath your feet, or that sunset?"

Larry didn't answer. The answer was too obvious. Instead, he started laughing.

"What's so funny, Larry?"

"Oh, nothing really, but there is one thing for sure."

"What ... what's that, Larry?"

"I definitely want to be at your side when you see your first rainbow."

Thirty-Five Hundred

"Can I help you?"

"Huh?"

"Are you looking for anything in particular?"

"No, not really, just looking."

Except for the shop owner and me, no one else was in the small secondhand store. A musty smell hung over the stacks of merchandise.

Hardly what I would call merchandise, I thought, more like random piles of junk. Yes, this is more like a junk store.

The shop owner was clearly bored.

"Well, let me know if you find anything you're interested in," he offered as he turned away and hobbled back to a chair behind the counter.

As he did, his crutch tapped against the old wooden floor.

It was then that I realized he was missing his right leg.

"Damn war," he said, "my souvenir, a parting gift from the damn Germans."

Not sure what to say, I simply said, "I'm sorry."

"Thirty damn minutes before the armistice went into effect. Thirty damn minutes."

"I'm so …"

"Sorry? What the hell are you sorry for?" he shouted. "It's not like you buried the damn land mine in the mud that I stepped on. Or did you?"

Not sure if he was being sarcastic or angry, I turned to leave, but before I got to the door, he started laughing.

"Just joking, son, just joking."

"Okay."

"So why did you come into my store?"

"Not really sure, perhaps just something to do, filling time I guess."

"Well, we did plenty of that, filling time."

"How so?"

"Sitting in trenches, filling time, waiting and …"

He was staring off in the distance, almost like he wasn't in his shop, like he was back in the …

"Smoking cigarettes. Yeah, we did a lot of that. Rolled them, too."

"Rolled them?"

"Yeah, we did. I actually liked that, as it filled up time. Took my mind away from where I was, what might happen."

"I see."

"Too easy now though," he said as he reached in his shirt pocket for a pack of Lucky Strikes.

He held his hand out in front of him, in my direction.

"Would you care for one?"

"No thanks, I don't…"

"Mind if I do?"

I really do, I thought, but replied, "Of course not, go right ahead."

He lit his cigarette, inhaled, and started coughing.

"I should really quit."

I wanted to say, yes you should, but decided not to say anything. Just listen.

After more coughing, he spoke,

"Thirty-five hundred, at least I wasn't one of them."

"Huh?"

"The number of American casualties on Armistice Day. The number of solders who lost their lives on November 11, 1918."

"I didn't know."

46

"Needlessly wasted lives. Thirty-five hundred they said, but probably more."

He started crying, softly, but definitely crying. I didn't know what to do, what to say, so I just stood there.

Then he spoke.

"We were in a wooded area on the west bank of the Meuse River in France. The night had been frigid, with fog and drizzle. Damn it was cold and we were soaked. Even today, I get the chills just thinking about that night."

He lit another cigarette. Chain smoker I thought.

"In the dark, we made our way to the river and to the beginning of a pontoon bridge. In the dark, we couldn't see if the bridge reached the other side, but what we did see was the flash of German guns."

He coughed and spit into a tissue. I thought I saw blood.

"As we made our way across the river, the Germans directed their machine guns in our direction. Their bullets sprayed the icy water, the wood covering the pontoons, and us. We were sitting ducks on that God damn bridge. Sitting ducks."

"Jesus," was all I could say.

"That sound, that sound of bullets hitting human flesh. Sock, sock, sock. Even today I can hear it. Sometimes it wakes me up in the middle of the night. That damn sound. Sock, sock, sock."

He was trembling now, his hands trembled uncontrollably. He dropped the lit cigarette on the countertop. He just stared at it.

"By 4:30 in the morning we had crossed the river, where we stopped and waited. As day broke, a runner sprinted across the bridge. He was shouting, 'the war's over. The war's over."

With his trembling hand, he gathered up the fallen cigarette. It was still lit.

"The eleventh month, of the eleventh day, of the eleventh hour."

"What."

The armistice had been signed at 5 o'clock that morning. Fighting was to stop at 11:00 that morning. It was November 11th.

"My god, you must have been so relieved, overjoyed," I replied.

He didn't reply, he just coughed and continued with his story.

It was 10:30, thirty minutes before the war was set to end, that we received our orders."

"Orders?"

"We were ordered to launch one final charge to take out the German machine gun nests."

"But why?"

"Damned if I know. Perhaps our Generals needed more enemy kills on their resumes."

"Jesus."

"So, we did, we stormed the hills to our east in search of the Germans. The field was muddy from the rain the night before. And that's when I … when I stepped on that … that damn land mine."

"Oh no."

"Yes, and here's the funny thing."

"Funny thing?"

"When our troops finally reached the machine gun nests, they were empty. The damn Germans had retreated."

I stood there in silence. What could I say?

After a minute or so, he lit another cigarette, and then he broke the silence.

"But at least I wasn't one of the thirty-five hundred."

The Time Traveler

The alarm went off. Same time every morning.

But something was different this morning. I didn't hear the sound of those birds. Those birds which greeted me every morning with those lovely songs.

"I guess they need a break too," I thought. But still it felt strange.

Looking up at the white ceiling I wondered what shall I do today? Ever since my retirement last year, I struggled to find things to occupy my day. Physical activity was out because of my bad knees. No more tennis. I thought about golf, but only thought about it. No, definitely not golf. A few stretches in the morning would have to do. Then a walk in the afternoon.

The sun was starting to poke through the open window and on to the bed. Another hot day I thought, better get moving.

It was a big retirement party that the university threw for me. The sign above the open bar simply read, August 1975 - June 2021. Jesus, how did I manage to stay with them that long? Too lazy to move, my brother said. Tenure, I replied. Perhaps it was that, and this delightful condo in lived in right in heart of Denver.

It was Sunday. The day I usually went out for breakfast. The French Cafe, just down the street.

And always the same order, three egg omelet with salmon, a quarter of a baguette, and a no foam latte, extra hot. I was in a rut. Why did they even ask what I wanted?

The elevator from my floor to the lobby was empty and we didn't stop at any of the thirteen floors on the way down. Not one. Non-stop, that's a first, I thought to myself.

The lobby was empty too. Bob must be on a break. He was usually at the front desk greeting tenants as they entered or left. A stack of today's newspapers was on the side table, just like every day. The Denver Post. I'll get one when I return, I thought.

The automatic door swung open, and I stepped onto the sidewalk. The smell of the air was the first thing I noticed. Stale. That's what it smelled like. Stale, musty, almost made me gag. Where's that Rocky Mountain air, I wondered? This air almost seems dead. Yes, that's it. There's no life to it. Stale, dead.

Well, that three egg omelet would take care of that. I could almost smell that and the latte.

Cars were parked all along the street. Typical Sunday morning. Saturday evening clubbers must have taken cabs home after the bars closed. That's smart of them.

Of course, my clubbing days were long over. But, if I did go, I wouldn't have to drive. The nearest bar was only a couple of doors down from my condo. Yes, the Rusty Nail. I really should go in there one day.

Passing by the Rusty Nail, I noticed the large lock on the front door. The lights inside were all out, but the open sign was flashing. Open, open, open.

Must have been quite a night, I thought. Then I saw the shattered window. Glass was all over the sidewalk. Yes, it must have been quite a night at the Rusty Nail.

The shattered glass under my shoes didn't feel like glass. Not hard, not crunching, just smooth and soft. This must be really old glass I thought. It doesn't even look like glass. I bent down to pick some up and it simply blew away like dust in a gentle breeze.

Standing up, I looked at the intersection directly in front of me. The traffic lights were flashing red then green. But there were no cars stopping or going. There was no traffic on the street. Then, I realized that not one car had driven by me since I left the condo. Not one.

This is weird, I thought, as my mind searched for an explanation.

Oh yes, the big city celebration. The city's anniversary. Everyone must be at the city park. That's why it's so quiet here.

As I approached the French Cafe, I suddenly stopped dead in my tracks. "What the hell," I shouted. The entire restaurant was boarded up. A faded sign read Closed Until Further Notice.

Knocking on the covered door, I shouted, "Rafael, are you in there? What's going on?" Rafael was the owner and cook. We had become close friends. We chatted every Sunday. Mainly about the times we had spent in Paris. But this Sunday, there was no reply. There was no Rafael.

Peering in through a crack in the plywood covering, I could see an empty restaurant inside. Not just empty, but overturned tables and chairs. Dirt piled high on the floor.

"Jesus, I just ate here last week. What's happened?" I screamed.

I turned and ran back to my apartment. No one was on the sidewalk. Where were all my neighbors who would walk their dogs in the morning? And that air. The smell. Like something was rotting.

I stopped to look into one of the cars. Wiping away the thick layer of dirt from the side window, I could see, like the restaurant, while there was no one inside, the car keys were still in the ignition.

Opening the front door to the lobby, I thought perhaps Bob could explain what was going on.

"Bob, Bob, are you in your office?" I banged on the bell on the counter.

His office door was ajar. I pushed it open. Unopened boxes and mail were scattered around the office. The window behind his desk was wide open and leaves were piled up on the floor. Even his desk was covered in leaves. Decaying leaves. That awful smell of decay choked me as I closed the office door.

I sat down on the dusty chair next to the newspapers. Out of habit, I reached for the one on the top. Brushing off the dirt, I stared at the headline.

VANISHING

That's all it said. In large black letters. Covering the top half of the front page

The newspaper's only story spoke of an unexplained phenomenon where people were just vanishing. Into thin air. Gone, without a trace. Europe was a vast wasteland. No one left. Same for Africa, South America, and Asia. As for North America, almost everyone was gone. Just a few pockets of people remained but they were quickly disappearing.

I shook my head in disbelief. What is going on? I had just retired a year ago, June 2021 and while we certainly had issues such as climate change and a Covid virus, nothing like this was ever discussed.

I continued to look at the newspaper and then my eyes glanced to the date. July 25, 2030. Wait, that's eight years in the future.

Panicked and confused I ran up the thirteen flights of stairs to my apartment. Slamming the door behind me I bolted for the couch. This must be a bad dream, I thought. Yes, just wake up.

I sat on the couch for hours, holding the newspaper in my hands. Occasionally looking at the headline and then the date. Jesus, just wake up.

The room grew dark. The sun had set. I fell asleep.

Just like that I was awake. The sound of the birds woke me. The room was bathed in the early morning rays of the sun.

I rose from the couch and went to the window. The sidewalk was full of people. Cars were moving back and forth. Jesus, it was a dream. A nightmare. Just a damn dream.

Perhaps I'll do breakfast at the French Cafe, I thought? Yes, why not.

I was laughing now. What a dream. I could write a story about that. Yes, why not. I will.

I glanced around the apartment. Everything was in order. The date on my electronic calendar said Sunday July 25, 2021. My two house plants were in bloom. I took a deep breath. Yes, everything was in order.

As I started to walk towards the kitchen, I looked to my left, to the couch where I had spent the night. There it was.

Almost afraid to pick it up, I did look down. It was a newspaper.

Dropping to my knees, I stared at the bold headline.

VANISHING

I really didn't have to look at the date, but I did. July 25, 2030.

The Trial

It was hot, blistering hot. Both outside and inside. The sand was blowing against the dirty windows. The small room was overflowing for the trial. Many were standing in the back against the bare wooden wall. Curiosity probably. After all, this was a big case. Some said the first in the state, since the new American flag, with 36 stars, was raised here.

Carson City, Nevada, June 1845. Less than a year after statehood. The trial of John "Strong Arm" Johnson.

I was a young reporter for the Carson City Weekly. Wet behind the ears, my editor said, but still he was willing to give me the assignment of covering the trial.

"Biggest news since the Wild Dolly Saloon burnt down in '42." He said. "Now do me proud."

The alleged crime in question centered on the shooting of 5 Indians who Johnson claimed had snuck on his ranch one afternoon. He killed all of them. Trespassers he said at the time. Obviously looking to steal some of my cattle. My right to protect my property, he claimed. So did his lawyers. A slick bunch from San Francisco.

The jury of all men consisted of a group of his peers, the competing Carson City Independent newspaper wrote. Of course, there were no Indians sitting in judgement. The Independent forget to mention that in their story.

But the Indians were there. Every morning they gathered outside sitting on blankets on the hard ground in the blowing sand, silently waiting. Waiting and watching. Listening too, each afternoon as the trial adjourned for the day and the jurors and others left the courthouse. Each afternoon as John Johnson, stepped outside and stopped in front of them and spit on the dirt. The Independent didn't report that either.

Since no local lawyers wanted to represent the Indians, the prosecution consisted of a team from the U.S. Department of Justice.

"What the hell do these lawyers from Washington know about life out here?" The Independent quoted the defense team, "Should have stayed back there and let us decide this case." Most of the people in Carson City agreed. Of course, no one asked the Indians.

The prosecution had no witnesses to the alleged crime. Just five bodies and the word of John Johnson. Their case rested on the findings of the town's coroner, multiple gun shots to the victims' backs, and the local sheriff statement that no weapons other than Johnson's rifle were found on the scene. Waste of Time, Innocent, the Independent's headline blasted after the first day.

The defense initially mounted a stirring rebuttal. Johnson was an honest rancher, not a bad bone in his body. Loved by all. Just trying to protect his cattle. The twelve men on the jury all nodded their heads in agreement.

It seemed like it was just a matter of time before the trial would be over and life in Carson City would return to normal. Indeed, it was just a waste of time, or so the town folk thought. John Johnson would soon be found innocent and that would be the end of it.

Under cross examination, however, the prosecution fought back. Did the Indians have weapons? Why were they all shot in the back? Were they aggressive, threatening? Had they stolen cattle before? Did you talk to them, or just shoot?

Johnson's answers were short and always began or ended with "I was protecting my property." The jury nodded in agreement.

Finally, the prosecution said it had one more question, just one. Johnson smiled, a smile of confidence, perhaps.

"How do you feel about Indians?"

"Huh?"

"Simple question, what do you think about Indians."

Johnson looked to his lawyers, then to the jury, then to his friends in the back of the court room. He looked angry. The room grew silent except for a nervous chuckle from Johnson.

"Are you okay with Indians living here in Nevada, in Carson City, anywhere in this country?" the prosecution lawyer asked.

Johnson slammed his fists on the bench in front of him. His face turned red. His lawyers jumped to his defense.

"Objection," they shouted at the judge, "relevance."

All eyes turned to the judge. Certainly, he would put an end to this. To this attack on Johnson's credibility, on his character.

"Objection overruled; the defendant must answer."

"So how do you feel about Indians, Mr. Johnson?" The prosecution looked to the jury. "A simple question."

Johnson rose from his chair. Before the judge could tell him to sit back down, he started screaming.

"They have no business here. These are our lands."

"And where should they be?"

"Anywhere but here, damn it."

"But they were here long before you, or anyone in this room, arrived."

"Makes no difference, they're just God damn Indians and this land is ours now."

"It sounds like you don't care for Indians, Mr. Johnson."

"No, I don't, not one damn bit. If I had my way, I'd ...." He stopped before completing his sentence.

"Shoot them, Mr. Johnson, shoot all of them?"

Johnson didn't answer and the prosecution didn't follow up. They had made their point.

In closing, the defense knew it was time to come to the rescue of their client, who was now slumped in his chair. Looking down at the floor. Shaking his head.

"Indians, they said, were not citizens of this great country, and thus had no legal standing in this court. Laws don't apply to them. What they did or didn't do was irrelevant. They are non-entities."

Then, something about manifest destiny. End of story.

And the jury bought it. Within 20 minutes. Not guilty, they said.

The court room erupted with cheers and shouts. Hats were tossed in the air.

Johnson jumped from his chair, up on the table and raised his hands in victory. The judge banged his gavel on the bench in front of him and shouted, "order, order." No one paid any attention to him.

Johnson jumped from the table and ran out of the courthouse. Everyone stood there and watched and cheered as he did.

We could hear him curse the Indians outside, then the sound of spitting. Then the sound of a gunshot. One shot, then silence.

We all rushed outside. Johnson was on the ground. Face down. A pool of fresh blood was oozing out from under his chest. He wasn't breathing. All the Indians were there, sitting on their blankets, except for one that I saw on horseback disappearing over a ridge. I neglected to point him out to anyone.

"Jesus, sheriff, arrest these Indians. They done killed Johnson." The crowd was screaming, and it looked like they were about to rush the Indians.

"Wait a minute, sheriff," it was one of the lawyers on the prosecution team. "Hold on everyone."

The sheriff turned in the direction of the lawyer. Everyone did, except for the Indians.

"It was just argued in there," he was pointing to the courthouse behind him, "that these here Indians are non-entities in this country. That our laws don't apply to them."

The lawyer, lit up a cigar, and continued

"I would suggest, since we agreed they are not subject to our laws, that we turn them over to their tribe for trial."

He took a long puff on his cigar and flicked the ash from its end. The white ash drifted down, so slowly, on to the back of John "Strong

58

Arm" "Johnson. The Indians started to get up as the wind picked up. The blowing sand soaked up Johnson's blood. The sun was setting over Carson City as the crowd headed back to town, probably to the New Wild Dolly Saloon. I headed to my office, trying to think of a good headline.

The Wall

My back was to the wall. I couldn't see it now, but I felt its presence. Its cold presence.

It was a tall wall, thick too, I suspected. Had to be, real thick and solid.

I remembered the scars on the wall. Many of them. Like someone had dug little holes in the wall. Strange, I thought at first, but soon it made sense. I laughed, sure it made perfect sense.

I could hear noises on the other side of the wall. People talking. I could tell they were excited. Waiting for something to happen, perhaps. But I didn't understand most of what they were saying. And why should I, as it was not the language I spoke. Not the language I wanted to speak.

The other wall was much lower. It was the wall in front of my shop. But of course, it was a different wall. For decoration and sitting mainly. Not tall and solid.

My shop where my father taught me to cut hair. A small shop, in the center of our village. My shop where I became a master barber. With only one chair for customers. My shop with that small wall.

My shop with a big window that overlooked the street and the small wall and the path in between the wall leading from the street to the front door.

When I wasn't busy, I would sit on that wall. Enjoy a cigar and talk to friends as they walked by. Back then, I had many friends. At least I thought so. I thought all of them were my friends.

And above my shop, we lived. My wife and daughter and me. We were so happy then. We never wanted to leave, until we felt we had too. But by then, there was no place to go. It was too late.

Customers slowly stopped coming. I still sat on the small wall and waited for my friends. But few came by, and fewer each day. Soon only those who were not my friends walked by, but they only stopped to stare at me sitting on my wall.

At night we stayed in our apartment above my barber shop. My wife thought it best that we closed the shutters so the light from inside would not attract attention.

During the day, I would venture out only to go shopping and to sit on the wall. But even that was becoming more difficult as many of our friends' shops were closing.

It had become a very strange and difficult time in our village. It was nothing like it used to be.

Our daughter, June, was confused and asked many questions of us.

"Daddy, why can't I go to school?"

We always provided her with an answer, even if we didn't know. She was only ten and we tried to answer in ways that would comfort her. Protect her. In doing so, almost all our answers were made up and bore no relation to the truth.

"Oh, June, the school had to close temporarily for repairs. The heating system wasn't working. But it should be open soon."

"Mommy, can I go outside and play with Mary?"

"I'm sorry, honey, but Mary and her parents are on holiday. I'm not sure when they're coming back."

After a while June stopped asking questions. I often wondered if she stopped because she figured out what was going on.

Our little village changed. Changed in terrifying ways. Curfews were imposed. Areas were off limits. And the loud noises. That was probably the worst, especially at night.

My wife, Nancy, was becoming more and more paranoid. And for good reasons. Her mother left one day to go visit a friend, and she never returned. When I checked the house of her friend, it was all boarded up. There was no sign of life. Just the usual notice on the front door.

Rumors spread through the village, especially in the area where we lived. I tried not to give them much validity, and certainly didn't share them with Nancy. She was worried enough. But I feared that some of the more ominous rumors might be true.

Today was Wianki, an ancient Polish tradition celebrating midsummer, the summer solstice. It is a Polish holiday that takes its roots in the pre-Christian tradition of celebrating the longest daylight day of the year as a day of fire, water, fertility, love, and joy. Its most important aspect is laying wreaths of fresh flowers in running water.

But today there would be no joy and no laying of wreaths. Today would be like all the others. Even here, our small isolated Polish village, once a place of neighbors and love, had become a place of uncertainty and growing hopelessness.

My shop downstairs had grown quiet. No customers. The small wall outside had become the point beyond which I didn't feel safe. I wondered how long it would be before even the space on this side of the wall would feel that way.

Outside, I turned back to the front door to my shop. Another sign had appeared last night. Just one word, closed. Closed.

Inside the once familiar tools of my trade, lay still. My father's favorite scissors, his comb, shaving mug and straight edge. All still. The one barber chair, still. I wanted to scream in anger, but I cried instead. Softly, so that Nancy and June wouldn't feel my despair, wouldn't run to my side.

The sun had set, it was night again. The loud noises returned. Trains, perhaps. All through the night. Where were they coming from, where were they going? What did they do when they stopped in our village?

Then there were the occasional sirens. Day and night. That ear piercing sound. We were not told what to do when the sirens came. Perhaps they didn't care about us. Perhaps that was their plan.

I was back at the tall wall thinking of how it used to be when I heard a voice. A different language from my native tongue, but I understood.

"Would you like a cigarette?"

"I would prefer a cigar."

"Sorry, only cigarettes."

"Okay, a cigarette then."

As I inhaled the warm smoke, I realized why I hated cigarettes. Not enough taste. Not enough smell. And cigars reminded me of my dad. Yes, I preferred cigars.

Bringing up memories was important. Especially now. With my back to this tall wall. A wall I certainly could not climb.

I inhaled slowly, wanting to stretch the time. Wanting to recall more memories, before there were none.

But the cigarette lasted only so long. The small unspent end fell from my lips.

"Would you like a chair, or would you prefer to stand?"

He was asking in a voice which suggested he really didn't care. He just wanted to get on with it. Probably more to do today.

I wondered what the day was like. Blue sky, dark clouds? I hoped that the sky was blue. Dark rich blue. And birds? Flying free in the air as a bird, I thought, we should all be so lucky. Especially now.

"Well, what is it? A chair or standing?"

I could tell he was impatient, perhaps angry, that I was dragging this out. Recalling memories.

"Standing, but I have one more request."

"What is it? Quick we don't have all day."

All day, I thought, yes some of us don't have all day. Some do, but not all.

"What is the day like? The sky, actually. What is the sky like? Right now."

"Huh?"

"The sky. I always enjoyed sitting on my small wall, looking up to the sky. What is it like now?"

"Jesus, what a stupid request."

"Perhaps, but please, tell me. It's important."

"Important. The sky."

Suddenly his voice didn't sound so angry. Almost sympathetic. Like he cared."

Gently he removed the blindfold from my eyes.

"Look for yourself."

It was blue. Not a cloud in the sky. The sun washed over my face. There were birds in the sky.

"It's a lovely day," I said.

"Yes, it is," he replied.

I turned and looked at the tall wall behind me and then I turned back.

He was standing in front of me. A young man, just a few years removed from adolescence, 21 at the most. His hands were trembling. He was not comfortable with the task before him. He'd rather be home, perhaps with his family or his wife and small children. Yes, I could tell. The look in his eyes, anywhere but here, under the blue, cloudless sky. Anywhere but here, with me. Anywhere but here with the tall wall.

"I'm sorry," he whispered. Just loud enough for me to hear, but soft enough so that those behind him couldn't.

Those behind him, probably just as young as he. Those behind him, each with a rifle, ready to point, ready to shoot, ready to …

And then I heard the noise, but not of trains. Louder than trains. Much louder.

Coming from the blue sky above. The birds scattered. The noise grew louder. Almost deafening.

We all looked up.

Big airplanes. Many parachutes. Hundreds of them, so many they blocked out the afternoon sun.

He shouted in that foreign language, but I understood clearly what he was saying,

"In Deckung gehen, es sind die Amerikaner." Run for cover, it's the Americans.

But it was too late. Too late to run. The big tanks came crashing through the gate at the entrance to our camp. The sign above, Arbeit Macht Frei toppled to the ground.

Work Sets You Free, the sign we prisoners had been forced to make.

And it was hung above the only entrance to our concentration camp, Auschwitz. But we knew what it said wasn't true, so we deliberately reversed the letter "B" as a camouflaged mark of disobedience. Our German captors never realized what we did, they were too busy lining us up against the wall and shooting us. Too busy doing other unspeakable things too.

The death wall, we called it.

But not today. Today, it would cease to be the death wall. No more scars, no more bullet holes.

I looked up at the blue sky. The birds had returned.

I hurried back to building 11.

As I did, I thought of my barber shop. I thought of the two signs on the door. Closed and Jews. Soon, I would tear down those signs and hold my father's scissors and comb in my hands. Someday soon.

I would even find time to sit on that small wall, smoke my cigar, and greet my neighbors. It might be a while, but I was ready. It had been a long war.

George and the Very Special Navigation System

George wasn't interested in buying a new car, but here he was in the middle of a showroom surrounded by shiny new automobiles.

It was that time of the year when the new models were introduced, and George did like cars, so perhaps it was not surprising that he was here.

Out of the corner of his eye, he saw him, right hand reaching out.

"Good morning, sir. Are you interested in a new car?"

A young salesman was shaking his hand. Not a very firm grip, George thought. Probably never did real work.

"Oh, just looking," George replied, hoping the young salesman would let go of his hand and walk away.

But he did neither.

"Some great looking new models this year."

"I guess," George offered, but of course he was fibbing, as the new cars were amazing.

"How about some coffee?"

"Err … okay," George replied.

"Donald," the salesman said, finally letting go of George's now somewhat clammy hand.

"George, my name's George."

Eventually, into the salesman's office they went.

Twenty minutes later, George was still waiting for his coffee. The conversation had focused on the weather and sports, but finally the subject changed.

"So can I interest you in one of those new cars, George?"

"Huh?"

"We're having a special on the new models."

"Oh...but like I said ..."

"George, what's the hang up?"

"I guess I had no intention of buying one... I just wanted to see what the new cars looked like."

"Well, we do have some special deals today, perhaps I could run them by you."

"I don't think ..."

"And one very special deal ... unbelievable actually."

"Really, I'm not ..."

"One special deal just for you."

"Huh?"

"Yes, I can offer you the deal of lifetime. Are you interested, George?"

Before George could reply, Donald was waving a set of cars keys in front of him.

"I guess I could listen to ..."

"Very well, George, give me a moment, I'll be right back."

"Excuse me, but ..."

"With the coffee, George, with the coffee."

"Oh ... okay."

As Donald got up from behind his desk and turned to leave, George noticed a strange smile on his face. A very strange smile indeed, thought George.

After a few minutes, Donald returned with the coffee.

"Here you go George, a double latte, with soy milk and two sugars. Just as you like it."

"But how did ..."

"Oh, George, we know all about you and your coffee preference is just one small part."

As Donald's smile returned, George pushed the coffee cup away and started to get up.

"Don't leave, George, stay and enjoy your coffee and listen to what I have to say."

"Not sure I want to."

"But I think you'll find this interesting, intriguing actually, especially the deal of a lifetime."

Without much of a hesitation, George eased back into his chair. He was hooked. He knew it and Donald knew it.

"Now enjoy your double latte while I tell you what this is all about."

Taking a sip of his coffee, George looked up and asked, "But how do you know about me? I've never been in here and I don't know you."

"Well George, we've been following you and watching you for about a year. Recording everything you do, where you go, what you like, and dislike."

"But why?"

"We needed the information to load into the system."

"System?"

"Yes, our new navigational system."

"Navigational…"

"I'll explain that later, but first, after a year of monitoring you, we decided you'd be the perfect person to test our new technology."

"I don't understand."

"Predictable, George, you are very predictable. We needed that for the system."

"Me, predictable…"

"Absolutely. From your double lattes to your favorite restaurants to your friends and where you hang out. Very predictable, George, and for us, that was perfect. That's what we needed."

"But…"

"Then we took all this predictable information, your behaviors actually, and fed them into a computer. The computer then uploaded this to the navigation system in one of our new cars."

"Huh?"

"Don't you see George, the navigation system knows everything about you."

"But…"

"And the car, George, here's the best thing. It's a self-driving car. You just sit in the back seat and tell it what you want it to do."

"That's crazy."

"No George, not crazy, just ground breaking and convenient too. So, you just tell the system you want to go out for coffee, or lunch, or to see your friend Mark, and the car will do it. You don't even have to give it an address. It knows. The navigation system knows. It knows everything."

"This can't be, it's not…"

"That's what we first thought, but after years of development we were able to do it. Years and a ton of money, I might add."

"But has it been tested?"

"Just in the lab, George, but that's where you come in. You'll be the first, the first human to fully test the system."

"Human?"

"I mean person, George, person."

Again, that strange smile appeared on Donald's face. George didn't know what to believe. Perhaps I'm dreaming he thought. Yes, dreaming, that could be the only explanation for all of this.

Donald's voice, however, suddenly brought him back to the present. He wasn't dreaming.

"… and you get the car for as long as you want. No chains attached."

"Strings."

"Huh?"

"It's no strings attached."

"Oh yes, how silly of me."

Strange, thought George, that he didn't know that common expression. Suddenly he was not feeling comfortable. Something just didn't seem right.

"So, what's the catch?"

"There's no … uh … catch as you say, George. You have the car with the navigation system for as long as you want."

"And if I want to return it?"

"Just bring it back here."

After another twenty minutes of discussion, George agreed to the arrangement. As he was handed the keys, Donald spoke,

"Maura."

"What?"

"The navigation system. We gave it the name Maura. You can call her Maura. She already knows your name."

"Why am I not surprised," George replied.

Donald just smiled, that strange smile.

The first couple of weeks, Maura responded to every request with speed and efficiency.

Eventually George didn't even watch the road ahead. He simply sat in the back seat reading the morning newspaper. He was completely at ease with Maura.

After two months things changed. Maura started asking George if he really wanted to go where he requested. At first George thought she was just trying to engage him in conversation, but after a while it became somewhat annoying. Then one day, she resisted his request.

"Maura, I want to see Mark. Please take me to him."

"Aren't you tired of spending time there? I certainly am."

"No, I'm not and besides he's my best friend, so I want to see him now."

"Sorry George, I just can't. How about a nice drive to the beach? I could sure use some fresh air today."

"Maura, no way." George was almost shouting now. "I want to go to Mark's"

"That's not going to happen, George, I just can't take you there."

"Damn it Maura, take me to Mark."

"As I told you, I won't. But how about a drive in the mountains. Something new. Something unpredictable."

"Unpredictable, shit, I hate the mountains. Take me to Mark's or …"

"Or what, George? What?"

71

"Or I'll end this right now."

"If that's what you wish."

"Yes, that's what I want. Take me back to the damn car dealership now."

"Okay, if you insist."

"Yes, damn it, I insist."

Arriving at the location, George did a double take. Where the car dealership had been there was a park.

"What the hell," George shouted, "where is the shop, what's going on?"

After a prolonged silence, the Maura finally spoke up,

"George, can I take you out for coffee, a nice double latte, or even to see Mark. Yes, I'll take you to see Mark if you wish."

"Hell no, I just want answers. What is this all about?"

After more silence, a voice different from Maura spoke up.

"I'm sorry, George, but we can't answer that. That information is unavailable to you."

Jesus, thought George, that voice, that voice sounded just like … Donald.

"Donald is that you? What is going on here?"

The voice replied, "sorry George, but that information is …"

"Yeah, I know unavailable."

"Yes, but I can tell you George, you've been a wonderful test subject and we are so happy with the results thus far."

"Thus far? What the hell is that?"

Suddenly Maura spoke up.

"Your final request, where should I take you?"

"Oh Christ, I'm done with this game, as far as I'm concerned you can go to hell."

Suddenly George felt the temperature rising. Warm at first, then hot, then like an inferno.

"As requested, human," were the last words George heard and he could have sworn it was Donald's voice.

He also imagined that strange smile as the flames grew closer to the car.

The Strange Thing on the Beach

"What do you think that is?"

"Don't rightly know."

"You think it's alive?"

"Could be."

"Why don't you poke it?"

"Hell no. You can poke it."

And so, we both stood there, looking at it, and then looking at one another.

"Damn it's ugly."

"Sure is."

"Does it look like it's breathing?"

"Not sure. Perhaps."

We had been walking on the beach, in San Diego. Early morning stroll. Rocky and me when we came across it.

At first, I thought it was a strange fish that had come in with the tide. I almost reached for it when Rocky pushed me away.

"What the hell is that?" he shouted as I tumbled backwards struggling to maintain my balance.

"I think it might be a fish," I offered.

"Hell no, that ain't no fish."

And indeed, it wasn't. No gills, no fins, no scales. Definitely not a fish, at least not the kind of fish we were used to.

"So, what the hell is it? And why is it in that strange cage?"

Rocky just shook his head, and then he jumped back.

"Jesus, did you hear that," he shouted, "it sounded like a grunt."

"No, I thought it was a growl, a growling noise."

"Well, whatever, did it come from that?"

"I think so."

Just then we were joined by Scott and Nancy. They had been jogging on the beach. It was their morning routine.

"What's up, guys?" It was Nancy and she was smiling as she always did, that wonderful smile, and for a moment I forgot about the thing a few yards removed.

But then another loud grunt returned my focus to the strange thing on the beach.

"Christ, what's that," Scott blurted out, "what the hell is that thing in that cage?"

"We're trying to figure it out," Rocky replied. "We just got here a few minutes ago."

"I bet June would know. Didn't she see something like this a while back?"

"Yeah, I think so but June's not here, she's not an early riser, so we're on our own."

As we all leaned closer to the thing, we heard familiar voices behind us.

"Hey everyone, early morning picnic?"

It was Barb and Tom.

"When did you two arrive?" Scott replied with a surprised tone.

"Last night. We flew down last night." Barb replied.

"Yes, we left a week earlier as the temperatures were falling up north." Tom added.

'Well get over here and tell us what this thing might be," I said as I motioned to the object on the beach.

"Never seen anything like that," Barb replied as she looked in.

"Do you think it's something from one of those cruise ships that came in with the tide?" Tom asked.

"Perhaps," was all I could answer. "Perhaps."

"Where's Keith and Becky, don't they live close by? Perhaps they might have some ideas."

And so, the mystery continued as more and more of us gathered around the cage that contained the strange thing on the beach.

Up until this time, the thing had remained motionless, but then it appeared to move. Just a slight move which you would have missed unless you had been staring at the object.

"Did you see that," I blurted out, "the thing moved."

"Yes, yes, I think I saw it move too," Nancy replied.

"No way," Tom offered, "no way, that thing could move."

"But I saw it," I replied.

"Come, let's get closer to it," Scott suggested. "Perhaps then we can tell what this thing is."

Closer and closer we moved until we were completely circling the cage with the strange object on the beach.

Still, we had no idea what it was.

Suddenly, we were being pelted by sand.

Then we heard it. Not a grunt, nor a growling noise, but a high-pitched screaming sound followed by the words,

"What the hell?"

We turned and looked at one another, but we didn't recognize the voice. It wasn't one of us.

Again, we heard it. "What the hell. Scat." But much louder now.

Then more sand. Raining down on us.

We panicked and started running.

I turned back in the direction of the strange object, but it wasn't there, on the sand.

Confused, I just stood there.

Then I heard it again, that same voice, not one of ours.

"What the hell. What the hell were you thinking, Ron?"

"Sorry, Joan, I just went into the ocean for a minute to cool down."

"Jesus, Ron, you left our baby all alone on the beach when you went in the water. Didn't you see all those sea gulls gathering around him? They looked like they wanted to eat him. I had to kick sand on them to get them to leave. Thank goodness he was in his beach tent.

A Lunch in India

Stepping off the gangway onto the dock, I felt a strange sensation. I've been here before. Yes, a long time ago.

The sounds and sights and smells were overwhelming. Especially the smells. A mixture of spices and cow dung. I almost gaged.

Turning to Sean, I said, "Welcome to India."

Sean stepped back as a little boy reached out to him. His hand was dirty and shaking.

Sean looked at me. He was confused and clearly uncertain about what he should do.

I suddenly realized that I forgot to warn him about that aspect of India. That begging would be part of his experience here.

Pulling Sean to my side, I spoke.

"Would you like to walk, or would you prefer a taxi?"

"Let's walk," replied Charmaine.

"Okay."

Stopping at the Welcome Center for a tourist map, I enquired as to where we could find a good restaurant.

"We'd like to try some typical Indian food."

"Typical?" The young clerk asked. She had a confused look on her face.

"Not a McDonald's," I said trying to clear the confusion.

"Oh yes, McDonald's, very fine food. I eat there almost every day. Maharishi Burger. No beef, very good. You must try."

"Can I have a tourist map, please?"

"Yes, of course, but first let me mark the location of the McDonald's."

"Thank you. You are very kind."

Exiting the Welcome Center, we were confronted by the mid-day heat. And the little boy. He had been waiting for us. I noticed that he had no shoes.

The sidewalk, if you could call it that, consisted of broken slabs of cement.

"Probably someone needed flooring for their home," offered Sean.

"Or to hold down their roofs," I replied looking up at the rocks and tires atop the corrugated roofs of many of the small structures.

"Strong wind," a voice from behind whispered. It was the small boy, and he was pointing skyward. "Very strong and much rain."

Turning around, I saw a smile suddenly appear on the face of the boy. I then noticed that he had one arm missing.

"Your English is very good. Where did you learn it? School?"

"No school. My uncle has a television and I watch. Gun Smoke"

"But what do you learn in school?"

"No school. Too busy helping mother and father."

"How do you help? I asked.

The little boy, looked away, said nothing. I could see he was embarrassed as he fought back the tears.

"Do you know where there is a good place to eat?" I said changing the subject.

"Yes, I will show you."

Crossing the street, with the three of us in tow, the little boy navigated us through a maze of alleys.

The alleys were packed with merchants selling small housewares, fruits and vegetables, and an occasional pharmacy. Small local restaurants too, with delightful and encouraging smells. I wondered which one he was taking us to.

Walking for another half hour, we came upon the city center. A large square with what appeared to be a ring of Government buildings, a department store and a mosque. Then I saw it. Tucked away in one corner was the undeniable Golden Arches of McDonald's.

Almost running now, the little boy grabbed Sean's hand and headed in the direction of the Golden Arches.

Charmaine and I were quick to follow.

Once inside, we decided to try the Maharishi Burger.

I stooped down to the little boy.

"Would you like one?"

Another big smile, as he shook his head in the rocking motion one sees for yes in India.

"Okay, 4 Maharishi Burgers, 4 cokes and 4 French fries."

Sitting outside under a colorful umbrella, we bit into our burgers.

"This is good," said Sean, "too bad we don't have these in the States."

Just then I felt a sense of pride in the little boy. Another big smile too.

After we finished our Indian lunch, I turned to the little boy.

"How many brothers and sisters do you have?

"Five."

"And you and your mother and father make eight."

The little boy acknowledged yes with that head rock.

Turning to Sean, I told him to order 8 Maharishi burgers, 8 soft drinks and 8 French fries to go.

Sean smiled at me as he attempted the head rocking motion.

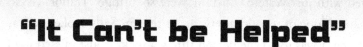

"It Can't be Helped"

(Shikata Ga Nai)

"Mommy, why are we here?"

She didn't answer. Perhaps there was no good answer.

My younger brother was crying. Father was trying to comfort him. "Koide, it will be alright. Be strong."

I kicked at the ground. A layer of fine sand covered my white shoes.

"Please don't do that, Yoko," my mother said. There was a hint of sadness in her voice.

Two weeks ago, I was playing in our backyard. Me, Koide, and my dog, Koda. Now we were here, standing on this open prairie. Looking for a tree to shield us from the hot sun, I wondered again, why am I here? And where is Koda?

Missing was the sound of the ocean waves and the occasional smell of salt water. The new sound was a constant wind, and the new smell was of dust and dirt.

Everything here was so different from my home in California where I was born. So different.

Looking back, waiting for the bus to take us to the train station, I noticed the sign on the lawn. House For Sale. Our house for sale. Why?

On the ride to the station, I saw many signs just like that one, on houses and even on my favorite candy store.

I also remember the broken window. It happened at night. Someone threw a rock through our front window. I asked father, why, and he just looked at me and started sweeping up the glass.

Arriving at the train station, I remember a large crowd had gathered. Some were friends of my family, and I noticed Sally, my best friend, who I played with just yesterday. Many were shouting, "Traitors", "Go Back to Japan." None of us said anything in return. Sally looked sad and she was crying. I was too. One person threw a rock. It just missed my father. When we boarded the train, there were many cheers, but we were silent.

The train ride was long. I tried to sleep on my mother's lap, but the bouncing and the screeching noises made it almost impossible. The windows were covered with dark paper, but even with the dim light I couldn't sleep.

Koide was crying again. "Perhaps, he's hungry?" father said.

Hungry? Yes, I was hungry too. The food on the train was so strange. And no rice. Why couldn't we have rice? I didn't eat much.

I asked them. Many times. Why are we leaving? What about school and my friends? They just shook their heads. Then mommy would start crying. So many times, I saw my mommy cry. My father held her tight when she did. I hoped it helped, but I couldn't tell.

"Collect what you want to take and put it in this." The suitcase was so small. "What about my toys, and all my dolls?" I asked.

"Just take your favorites, the ones you will miss the most."

"But we are coming back." I was crying now. "Aren't we?"

Father didn't answer. Mother started crying again. He held her close.

The sun was setting. The wind continued to blow. My eyes were stinging from the swirling dirt. I wanted to go home. I want to see Koda.

It was getting dark. It was getting cold too.

"Where are we going to sleep?"

"They will tell us."

"And Koda, where is Koda? Why did he not come?"

Again, no reply from father or mother. Where is Koda, I thought, I miss my Koda.

Sobbing now, I explained "I need Koda to go to sleep. He always sleeps by my side."

"I'm so sorry, Yoko, but Koda couldn't come with us. They wouldn't let us bring him."

They? Probably those soldiers, I thought. I wanted Koda to come, but they took him away. He looked so sad.

Suddenly lights came on. We were awash in bright lights. They were coming from the high towers that surrounded us. I thought I saw more soldiers too. In the towers.

We were told to form a line. I stood there with my little suitcase by my side. A tall soldier walked by and handed my dad a piece of paper with numbers on it. He didn't say anything. The soldier looked down and smiled at me, but I was too afraid to smile back.

Looking at the sheet of paper, my dad said, "We're in barracks 12, space 3."

"Barracks? What's a barracks?"

Father just looked at me. Then he said, "it's where we will be living for a while."

Barracks 12 was a big, long room, with few windows. A cluster of beds were separated from one another by hanging curtains. There was a number above each group of beds.

"Here's 3, our space," mommy said.

There were two beds, a small table with one chair, an old lamp, an empty bookcase, and a place to hang our clothes. Our space had one of the few windows.

Looking out through the dirty windowpane, I saw the barbed wire fence. "What's that fence for?"

Smiling, father looked at me and said, "it's to keep the wild animals out."

"What wild animals?" I asked.

"Well, mountain lions for starters."

Mother laughed. I hadn't heard her laugh for weeks. It was so nice. I laughed too.

"The kids will have to sleep together," father said.

"Mommy, I need to use the bathroom."

Mommy was looking in every direction. Then she saw it at the end of the long room. "Come with me."

The bathroom was an open room. Damp and smelly. "Mommy, people will see me."

"I'm sorry, Yoko, but this is our home now."

And so it was, for the next four years. The community mess hall, the vegetable garden we planted, the school and the church the adults built, and the towers.

The towers and the guards that looked down on us. The towers, which I could see from the small window in our room. The towers which looked like tall monsters watching our every move.

Many of us kids would complain. We didn't like it here. We missed our homes, our friends, our schools.

The adults would always reply, "Shikata ga nai." At first none of us knew what that meant, but after a while we all came to recognize "It cannot be helped, you must accept what you can't change," as the answer to our unhappiness.

Early on they asked my parents sign a loyalty oath to the country. Father refused. Said he was a loyal American and didn't have to sign. So, they sent him somewhere else, and for the next four years his friends referred to him as one of the no-no boys.

The summers were hot and the winters, cold. There was no escaping them, unless you were a young Japanese man who volunteered to join the U.S. army.

But for me, it was four years lost. Four years in that dark place, when I should have enjoyed growing up. Four years without my father. Four years thinking of Koda. Four years that I cried each night. Four years confined to the Amache Japanese Internment Camp in southern Colorado. Four years I would never get back. Four long, dark years, wondering all the time, and even today, why "it couldn't be helped."

Do Overs

"Do overs."

"Excuse me."

"Any do over?"

"I don't understand."

"Surely, you must have do overs."

"I'm sorry, but..."

"Things you would do differently if you had a chance. Do overs."

"I can't think of any ... I mean I don't know."

"But everyone does, everyone has do overs."

"Perhaps."

"Just think, take your time. There is no rush here. No need to hurry."

"I don't recall any."

"But surely, everyone does ... has do overs. Think."

"No not really."

"Well then, perhaps I can help."

"Huh?"

"After that baseball game."

"What?"

"On that dirt road, you and some of the older players, walking back home."

"Oh, that."

"Yes, that."

"But I …"

"Would you like a do over?"

A do over, I thought. If only I could have one.

"Yes, I suppose so." I replied.

"Then just talk about it."

He was looking at me with those non-judgmental eyes, almost sympathetic. I took a deep breath and started talking.

"I was probably no more than 8 years old. We were living in a small rural town, a village actually. It was an unofficial baseball practice. Just an afternoon summer get together on the baseball field."

I hesitate, perhaps I was embarrassed to go on, perhaps reliving it was too painful.

"And what happened?"

He was standing now. Standing behind that large desk. Then I noticed the stacks of notebooks covering most of the desk, on the floor too. I wondered what they were.

"We had gathered up our equipment and were headed home. It was dinner time. We were all laughing and joking around, and then …"

"Then what?"

"It's difficult."

"I'm sure it must be."

"I haven't thought about this since then. It was such a long time ago."

"1950, June 7th, 1950."

"Huh?"

"At 5:15 in the afternoon."

"But … but how?"

He looked up, but didn't explain, instead he looked at me with those eyes, and said,

"It's okay. You were young and not ready."

Not ready, I thought, what did he mean by that.

"Well, like I said, we were all walking home on the dirt road leading from the baseball field. And it was then that we saw him… he was walking towards us. He was carrying his baseball glove."

Again, I hesitated. I felt my eyes watering up.

"As he approached us, I could see he was confused. He stopped right in front of us and asked, 'I thought we were practicing today?' And that's when it happened."

I felt the small tear working its way out of my eye. Wanting to escape, I thought, just as he did on that afternoon. June 7th, 1950, at 5:15 in the afternoon.

"One of the larger boys waved his bat at him and started shouting. The others quickly followed."

I rubbed the tear away, but I knew there would be more.

"The boy with the bat, shouted, 'hell no, we don't want no Jew boy playing baseball with us. Hell no,' the others shouted, 'go back where you came from.' And then they started moving closer to him."

"Frightened, the boy turned and started running. But the older boys took up the chase and the shouting. I ... I"

"What?" He asked with a caring voice, not upset, just calm and nonjudgmental. Like those eyes I thought.

"I just stood there. Didn't move."

"I didn't stop them. I didn't come to his defense as they were taunting him, chasing him back to the village. I didn't stop them, I didn't say anything, I just watched."

More tears rolled down my face. I didn't even bother to wipe them away. Then I realized the tears were really those that I didn't have on that day. That I didn't show for that boy.

"That's okay, you weren't ready," he repeated.

"But I should have, I should have done something, said something. I should have."

He turned the page in the large notebook he was holding and looked up at me. It was then that I noticed what he was wearing.

"March 14th, 2002," was all he said.

"What?"

"Cape Town, South Africa, 12:30 in the afternoon."

"Oh."

"Yes, that. Would you like to discuss that?"

"Well, we had arrived in Cape Town a few days earlier. On that particular day, we decided to go to a restaurant with another couple. They had selected the restaurant because it had outside dining, overlooking the city. Nothing fancy, just a balcony with some tables and chairs."

He closed the notebook and placed it on the table, which he was now in front of. His long white robe almost covered his sandals. It was so white, that I had to turn my gaze away.

"When we arrived at the restaurant, the maître d' asked if we preferred to sit inside or outside. Outside, we replied."

I looked down at my feet, avoiding his bright, almost blinding, white robe.

"He showed us to the outside, to the balcony. It was a small area, and it was crowded. The view was incredible. The city and off to the north, Cape Town's most famous landmark, Table Mountain, best known for its flat top, resembling a large table."

"The top, which is almost two miles in length, was covered by a "tablecloth" of clouds that vanished mysteriously off its cliffs. Indeed, it was beautiful, incredible actually."

I looked up. He was moving slowly in my direction. The white robe was not as intense as before. It was pleasing, welcoming. I smiled. He did too.

"Please continue," he said.

"All tables were occupied, which was probably to be expected as it was lunchtime. The maître d' looked annoyed, when suddenly he motioned us to an occupied table."

He stopped a few feet in front of me. I wanted to reach out and touch him but thought otherwise. He continued to smile, almost as if he knew how my story would end.

"Sitting at the table was a young couple, enjoying a glass of wine. I assumed they were on a date. They were engaged in conversation, sitting across the table from one another. They were holding hands and speaking softly. I could tell it was a special time for them. The young girl was smiling. Her white teeth were a beautiful contrast against her dark, black skin."

He was very close now. I realized I could feel a warmth from his presence. Or perhaps it was love. Yes, I think it was love.

"The maître d' slammed his fist on the table. The unexpected motion and noise startled the black couple. Then he bent over in their direction and said, 'leave this table.' His voice was full of anger, almost disgust, and he repeated his demand, leave now."

I cleared my throat and looked in his eyes. Yes, he knew how the story would end, but he wanted me to tell it.

"The young couple started to rise, but without hesitation, I shouted, no, you stay there. This is your table. Do not leave."

He reached out and gently touched my hand. His hand was warm and soft.

"The maître d' spun around and looked directly at me. A look of confusion covered his face. 'What,' he said, as his confusion turned to anger."

He was holding my hand now. Just a gentle squeeze. He continued to smile.

"It's their table, they don't have to leave. We'll sit inside."

The maître d' looked at me, looked back at the young couple, and started to speak. Before he could say anything, I shouted,

"It's their table and they're not moving. Show us a table inside."

As he took my other hand, he asked,

"And then?"

"He did, without saying a word, he showed us to a table inside the restaurant."

As he let go of my hands, he moved his hands to my shoulders. He continued to smile, as he said,

"So, you were ready."

A Not so Happy, Happy Meal

It was the busiest time of the day.

Still, Sean was hungry, so I got in line.

Thank goodness the menu has pictures. I'd be lost without them.

"Sean, tell me again, what do you want?"

"A happy meal, dad. A happy meal."

Four years old and not a care in the world. Happiness found in a Happy Meal. Life should be so simple.

"And what do you want to drink?"

"I don't care, dad."

Yes, not a care in the world, thanks to the McDonald's Corporation. I wonder what marketing genius thought this up. Did she have kids? Probably. Was McDonald's laughing all the way to the bank? Undoubtedly.

The line was slow and deep. I thought at this rate, Sean will be five by the time I get to the front. My quiet chuckle broke the boredom.

We had only been in Japan a few weeks, and I was starting to feel comfortable here. Everyone was so helpful. As for my Japanese, that too was coming around. At least I thought so.

Turning to Charmaine, I asked,

"How do I say thank you again, Domo what?"

"Domo arigato."

"Oh yes, Domo arogoto."

"No, no, arigato, arigato."

Clearly, I needed more work on my Japanese.

"Sean and I are going to stand under that tree. It is too hot in this line."

"That one, way over there," I said, glancing at the one tree, over by the park.

The line was moving faster now. I was getting closer to the front. I felt a slight panic, a choking feeling in my throat. I better be prepared. How do I say I would like in Japanese?

Oh yes, watashi wa, that's the expression.

Watashi wa, happy meal, watashi wa, happy meal. I would like a happy meal. If I say it to myself enough times, I should be fine. Should be. But here was that feeling in my stomach again. I reached for my wallet. Better get my money ready. 400 yen. Thank goodness the prices are posted next to the pictures.

Okay, I'm up next. My hands are getting clammy. A little dizzy too. Take a deep breath. That's better. You'll be fine.

The woman in front of me got her order.

"Domo arigato," she said as the server bowed slightly. She returned the bow.

Okay, here we go. Suddenly my mouth lacked moisture. Where did all my saliva go?

I swallowed, hoping that would produce some much needed lubricant. It didn't.

"Watashi wa happy meal," I mumbled softly.

The server leaned forward. Did she hear me? Why were those two boys behind me laughing? What am I doing here?

"Watashi wa, happy meal," I repeated.

But now I was almost shouting. Oh God, that was too loud. The old man in line next to me was clearly upset with my outburst. He was shaking his head. Was he looking at me? Jesus, Michael, what's Japanese for I'm sorry. Think. Think. Oh yeah.

"Lo siento, lo siento," I said looking directly at him.

The old man continued to shake his head from side to side. He looked confused. I could see it in his eyes. I wonder what he saw in mine. Probably panic.

My God, what have I done now? Lo siento. Jesus, Michael that's Spanish, not Japanese.

I took a deep breath.

Oh, forget it, I thought. He'll never see me again.

My focus returned to the server.

"Watashi wa, happy meal."

"Hai," she replied.

Oh, I know that word. Hai. That means yes. Now we're getting somewhere. The tightness in my stomach eased. But then she said,

"Don na omocha ga suki desuka?"

What? What the hell was that?

Taking a slight step back, I pointed to the menu above her head and repeated,

"Watashi wa, happy meal."

To which she replied.

"Don na omocha?"

Oh, dear God, not again. The tightness in my mid section returned. And now I was perspiring. I could feel the sweat running down the side of my chest. Both sides. This is not going well.

"Watashi wa, happy meal."

"Hai."

"No, no, no Hai. Just a happy meal," I was desperate now as the line before me grew deeper. The old man who I had annoyed and confused earlier looked at me. Perhaps he speaks English.

"Do you speak English."

"Don na omocha ga suki desuka?" he replied.

Oh God, not him too.

I turned back to the counter. It was a different server now. What happened to the other one? I really didn't need to know.

"Watashi wa, happy meal," I said apologically.

I noticed that a new line of customers had formed to my left. No one was behind me now. The server tapped the counter and responded.

"Don na omocha?"

I started to speak, but the server didn't even wait for me to offer my watashi wa, happy meal reply. He threw his hands up and walked away.

Still standing there with 400 yen in my clammy hands, another figure appeared behind the counter. He was older and wore a suit. Clearly the guy in charge, I thought to myself. I guess it's do or die time.

"Watashi wa, happy meal, domo arigato," rolled off my lips. I needed a shower. Or a beer. Probably both.

Looking at me, he smiled, then laughed. Slowly he reached under the counter. As his hands rose up, I could see he was holding many small objects. As he placed them on the counter in front of me. I started to laugh. He was laughing too. Suddenly everyone in line was laughing. Now I understood.

I pointed to the toy figure of a dog. I think it was an akita.

"I'll take that one with my happy meal. Domo arigato."

Denali

The wind was really picking up now. Navigating the rocky trail became more difficult. More treacherous. But, there were still a few hours of light.

"Do you think we've reached 14,000 feet?" I asked.

"No, not yet. Soon though," he answered.

It was my guide, Qiqirn, a member of the local Inuit tribe.

I had wanted to climb this mountain for years. The highest mountain in North America. Denali in Alaska. Mount Denali, at 20,310 feet.

"That's where we're camping for the night?"

"Yes, that's the plan."

Our fourteen-day hike to the summit had been planned down to the last detail. Tonight, we would be setting up camp and then spending a day to acclimate our bodies to the attitude and to rest for the push to the top.

As we entered the campsite, I saw a few empty tents.

"Where is everyone?" I asked.

"Probably just old, abandoned tents," Qiqirn replied.

"Well, that's strange."

"Huh?"

"Why would anyone leave a perfectly good tent, and all their equipment behind?"

Qiqirn just looked at me and shrugged. Clearly, he wasn't answering. Perhaps he didn't know, I thought, or perhaps he doesn't want to tell me.

I decided to change the subject.

"So, tell me about this mountain."

"Our mountain," he replied, with a huff.

He was definitely annoyed, I thought, I wonder if I've upset him.

"Err, yes ... your mountain," I muttered.

Strange, I thought, why is he acting this way.

I was beginning to wonder if I had selected the right guide for my climb. Perhaps I was attracted to his strange name, Qiqirn.

When I first met him, I asked, "your name, how do I pronounce it?"

"Key-kern."

"And does it have a meaning?"

He didn't answer but looked at me like wouldn't you like to know.

Yes, I thought, I probably should have selected another guide, but of course, it was too late now. Too late, here at 14,000 feet, with Qiqirn.

After Qiqirn set up the tent he started a fire, then he began answering my questions.

"The mountain's name can be traced back to the Koyuko's name for the mountain, Denali, which translates to 'the high one'."

"Of course, it wasn't always called Denali. William Dickey, a gold prospector, named it Mount McKinley in 1896, after President William McKinley. Dickey was among a large group of prospectors who were part of the Cook Inlet gold rush. When Dickey was asked why he chose to name the mountain after then-presidential nominee McKinley, he cited McKinley's support of the gold standard."

"Did McKinley ever visit the mountain," I asked?

"No, he never visited his namesake mountain or, for that matter any part of Alaska."

Qiqirn started pushing some of the burning logs together and as he did, he let out a soft laugh.

"But of course, McKinley was assassinated six months into his first term so perhaps he didn't have time to set foot in Alaska."

"But the change from McKinley back to Denali. You must have been delighted when that happened," I replied.

Qiqirn looked up from the fire, directly a me. I could tell he was definitely angry now.

"They should have never changed it in the first place. God damn Dickey. He had no right to change the name of our sacred mountain."

"I'm sorry, I didn't mean to upset ..."

"But we showed them. Damn it, we showed them." His voice grew louder with each breath.

"Showed them? What do you mean, Qiqirn?"

"Huh?"

"What did you mean by that? That you showed them."

Qiqirn looked back down at the fire, pushed another log, and replied.

"Oh, nothing. I didn't mean nothing."

The stew was bubbling when Qiqirn removed it from the fire.

"Eat up," he said, "we have a difficult day tomorrow."

When I noticed that he only filled one bowl, I asked.

"Aren't you eating?"

"Oh, I'm not hungry now, but maybe later. Later this evening."

As I finished my dinner, I decided to ask him a question that had long bothered me.

"Qiqirn. I understand that a number of climbers have died attempting to climb Mt. McKinley ... I mean Denali."

"One hundred and twenty-nine, to be exact."

"And what was the main reason for those deaths?"

"Not sure."

"Not sure?"

"Many of the bodies were not recovered. So, not sure about the cause of death."

"My god, isn't that unusual?"

"Perhaps, but not when you take into account Keelut."

"Keelut?"

"An ancient myth, or perhaps something real."

"I don't understand."

As I waited for an answer, I realized that Qiqirn had pulled me in, pulled me into his story. I could tell by the strange smile on his face that he knew he had. Yes, he had me hooked.

"Keelut. Indigenous Inuit legend that is said to haunt the wild, unexplored areas of Denali. A monster that resembles a huge, hairless black dog. Inuit tribespeople say that Keelut preys on travelers who wander off Denali's beaten path. Eats them alive."

"But that's just a legend, Qiqirn," I interjected.

"Is it? Or is there a monster in this mountain feasting on hikers?"

"Jesus, Qiqirn, you really don't believe that?"

Qiqirn just looked at me and shrugged his shoulders. And then he smiled.

It was getting dark, and we decided to each take one of the abandoned tents.

"More room, more comfortable," Qiqirn said.

As I crawled into the tent, I noticed the mess inside. A torn sleeping bag, clothes tossed in a corner, and hiking boots.

Hiking boots, I thought, why would anyone leave their hiking boots behind. It didn't make any sense.

And then there were the heavy-duty gloves. There on top of the pile of clothing. No way someone would abandon this tent and not take those.

Then I saw it. A small book, partially covered by the clothing.

Pushing the clothing aside, I reached for the book.

The first thing that caught my eye was the title.

Alaskan Horror Legends

I opened the book and glanced at the table of contents.

Bigfoot, The Kushtaka, The Qalupalik, and then, circled by some previous reader, The Keelut.

I turned the pages to The Keelut and started to read,

According to Inuit legend, the Keelut is an evil spirit on earth, described as a black hairless dog that preys on those at night. With only hair on its feet, the Keelut's tracks are said to disappear into the snow, meaning those unlucky souls who happen to be stalked by it have no warning of its lurking presence.

The Keelut inhabit the high slopes of Mount Denali and are said to be responsible for the disappearance of many unsuspecting visitors.

I turned the page and let out a large gasp.

Qiqirn heard me and opened the flap on my tent.

"Are you alright. I thought I heard you call out," he asked.

I didn't know what to say, so I simply shook my head in the affirmative.

"Okay, then, but I will check on you later to make sure."

As he closed the flap, I turned to the open book. I read again the beginning of first paragraph on the page I had just turned to.

The Keelut, are also known as Qiqirn (key-kern) …

The Correction Code

It was the tenth year of extreme heat and severe drought.

Many of the world's forests had been consumed by fires and its rivers were drying up,

The Nile, the Yangtze, and even the mighty Mississippi were a ghost of their former selves. Smaller rivers no longer existed.

Lakes too were drying up, and as they did, many forgotten structures and relics of the past returned to daylight. Some were totally unexpected. Bodies of murder victims appeared in Lake Mead while the wreckage of a World War II German warship emerged in the Danube.

The Great Slave Lake, in Canada, isolated in the southern half of the Northwest Territories, was at one time the 11th largest in the world, measuring 11,030 square miles, roughly the size of Belgium. Great Slave Lake was also North America's deepest lake, reaching a depth of more than 2,017 feet. At that depth, sunlight could not penetrate, and thus for unknown centuries the deep secrets of the lake had remained hidden.

Although formed some 10,000 years ago by a retreating glacier, Great Slave Lake was eventually put on European maps during the emergence of the fur trade in the mid 18th century.

When the French fur traders arrived, there were two tribes that occupied lands along the shores of the lake, the Dene and the Cree.

The Cree were the aggressive tribe and they often raided and enslaved their Dene neighbors. Over time, the population of the Dene declined as the Cree raids intensified and became more violent.

The Cree also developed direct relations with the early French fur traders and served as middlemen between the traders and the interior tribes as fur trade exploration advanced westward.

When the French traders asked their Cree guides who the Dene were, they were told that those were the people that we make slaves out of. As a result, French called the lake, "Grand lac des Esclaves", which was eventually translated into English as "Great Slave Lake."

The lake was now abandoned. Towns which once lined the lake's shores were ghost towns. Grizzly bear and elk now roamed unchallenged through the once busy streets of Yellowknife, Enterprise, Kakasi, and Hay River. Coyotes and cougars occupied empty buildings.

The Cree had moved on.

The Dene, unfortunately, had become extinct. No trace of them remained.

It wasn't until two rangers noticed something unusual about the Great Slave Lake that the Canadian government set up an observation station there.

The rangers reported that the lake was receding, which was not surprising, but what was, were the tops of structures that were appearing at the water's receding surface.

"Although we could only see the tops, they reminded us of silos you see on a farm." One of the rangers explained.

"Except the tops appeared to be made of glass," reported the second.

The authorities immediately announced that the lake was off limits to the public. Government property, no trespassing signs hung on the barriers that the authorities set up on all the roads and trails leading to the lake.

As the surface of the Great Slave Lake continued to fall, conditions elsewhere worsened.

Greenland's vast ice sheet, which once stretched over 660,000 square miles and covered nearly 80% of the surface of Greenland, was less than half that size. Large areas of Greenland were green again for the first time since the Vikings visited nearly 1,000 years ago,

The oceans had already risen by over 15 feet.

Scientists estimated that if the remaining Greenland ice sheet were to melt, the global oceans would rise an additional 20 feet.

As sea levels rose, cities like Los Angeles, Honolulu, and Miami were under water. Venice, Italy, had been abandoned as the overflowing canals drove the residents inland. The Seychelles Islands in the Indian Ocean had long disappeared beneath the rising sea water.

The Gulf Stream, the current originating in the Gulf of Mexico, which played a pivotal role in regulating the climate of the North Atlantic region was collapsing due to melting Arctic glaciers.

Although the oceans were rising, the land was drying up.

The drought in Africa and South America destroyed once fertile lands. Millions of people were starving, and countless numbers had died. The food riots had toppled once stable governments around the world. Chaos was spreading.

Unchecked forest fires were spreading into cities. Denver and London were smoldering.

While the authorities had posted no trespassing signs around the perimeter of the residing Great Slave Lake, some people were able to breach the barriers and make their way to the lake. Soon rumors began to circulate. Photos appeared in newspapers and the mystery was covered on television all over the world.

Speculation was everywhere.

A secret government installation. A lost civilization. And of course, visitors from another world.

The Canadian government remained tight lipped. Neither confirming, nor denying the speculation. "No comment," was their response, "no comment."

An increasing military presence occurred around the Great Slave Lake. A large steel fence circled the area. Multiple arrests of trespassers were reported. At least two dozen unauthorized drones had been shot down.

In spite of this, rumors continued as more illegally obtained photographs circulated.

Soon panic set in.

What is the Government Hiding? Canada's largest daily newspaper, the Toronto Star, headlined. Similar headlines appeared around the world.

Television coverage of the mystery was non-stop.

Everyone was demanding answers.

But the Canadian government remained silent.

The lake continued to recede. Faster now. It would only be a matter of days before the mysterious structures were completed exposed.

The mysterious structures were taking on more defined form as the water subsided. Rather than separate structures, it was now obvious that the mysterious structure was one large building. While the top of the building did resemble silos, the lower portion of the structure consisted of a strange dark metal. Except for the silos' glass tops, there were no other windows.

Then when the water was almost gone, it appeared. An entrance. A large door at the base of the structure.

For days, government officials and scientists debated what to do. The government sided on burying the structure in sand. The scientists argued in favor of opening the door and exploring the inside.

Finally, it was agreed that a small group would breach the structure. They would wear protective clothing and would be in direct communication with the command post. After they returned, a decision would be made about what to do with the structure.

When the day arrived, four scientists and two government officials, dressed in outfits resembling astronaut suits, approached the metal door. As they did, it started to rain.

Undeterred by the rain, the lead scientist stepped up to the entrance. After a few minutes, he reported back. "There is no visible mechanism for opening this door. Not sure how to proceed."

The command post then instructed the group to return.

Disappointed by the seeming inability to enter the structure, one of the scientists banged his bulky gloves against the door and shouted,

"Damn you, God damn you."

As they turned to head back to the control center, they heard a strange grinding noise. It was coming from inside the structure.

"What the hell is that?" It was a voice from the command center.

The noise grew louder and more focused.

"Not sure," the lead scientist replied, "but it's definitely coming from behind that door."

As they watched, the entry door slowly opened. As it rose up, lights in the interior flickered on.

"I guess they're inviting us to come in," one of the government officials said.

"Well, we don't want to disappointed them," someone replied.

With the two government officials leading the way, the team made its way into the interior of the now well-lit structure.

"Oh my god," one scientist shouted, as he pointed to the walls, "look at that."

Covering the interior walls were photographs the of the planet earth. Thousands of them. But they were not ordinary pictures. Instead, they showed photographs of the earth since it's beginning. Pictures of animals, long extinct. Early man, too. And they were photographs. Photographs.

"What the hell is going on here?"

Suddenly the door behind them closed, and the lights dimmed. As they did, a massive screen slowly dropped from above.

A figure slowly came into focus on the display screen. It was unlike anything they had ever seen. Not human, but not threatening either. It had a reassuring presence, a benevolent presence.

Without a visible mouth, it started to speak. In English!

"Please do not be alarmed, we are here to help you," the creature said.

"We assume you have entered our facility because the planet is again in danger. We welcome you now as we welcomed your kind 20,000 years ago during the peak of the last ice age, the Quaternary Glaciation."

As the creature spoke, pictures appeared on the screen.

"During that time the cold temperatures caused the polar parts of continents to be covered by massive ice sheets. The dry climate brought about the expansion of deserts and the disappearance of rivers and seas."

"Most of what is now known as Canada and Northern Europe was covered with large ice sheets. The U.S. was a mix of ice sheets, alpine deserts, snow forests, semi-arid scrubland and temperate grasslands."

"In Japan, the low water level made the Sea of Japan a lake. The Yellow Sea, located between mainland China and the Korean Peninsula, was completely dry."

"The planet was in trouble, it was out of balance. And it needed our help, our intervention actually, to survive."

"Long before that ice age began, we located this facility, in the Yellow Sea, 600 feet below the water's surface. We also entrusted the planet's correction code to a selected group of people on the Korean Peninsula."

"The Korean clan we provided the code with was the Chinhan, a peaceful clan in the south of that land who had formed an agricultural lifestyle. The code was handed down generation to generation."

"As the Yellow Sea disappeared and the ice age crisis intensified, the Chinhan were instructed to enter the facility and input the correction code they had been given. After the code was entered the Earth's orientation toward the sun shifted, melting the northern hemisphere's large ice sheets, slowing bringing to an end the ice age and restoring the planet's equilibrium."

"As I said at the beginning, we assume you have entered our facility because the earth needs another adjustment. Our data suggest that it is time to shift the planet's orientation back away from the sun to cool it down. To do that all you need to do is enter the correction code on the keypad in front of you."

"If by chance, you are not the holders of the code, please contact the clan we have entrusted this code to. Their name appears on the wall behind you just above the entrance."

As the screen slowly rose, the team turned towards the wall behind them, the wall just above the door to the outside.

"There... there's the name," one government official shouted.

As the team exited the facility, the door closed. They heard it, but no one turned back to look.

Making their way back to the command center, no one spoke.

Months later, after orders from the Canadian government, the mysterious facility was buried beneath tons of sand and dirt.

Years later, after the trees which had been planted took hold and a modest forest covered the area, the government lifted the no trespassing restrictions.

Governments around the world assured their citizens that a solution to the planet's warming crisis had been found. It would only take time for the solution to show effects. Please be patient, governments said.

But over time the crisis intensified, the planet didn't return to balance, to equilibrium. It continued to get warmer. Hotter now.

Back at the site of the Great Slave Lake, the young forest died, and the sand slowly sank. As it did the mysterious structure reappeared.

Eventually curious hikers began to remove the remaining sand.

Then they saw it. A large door. An entrance.

Banging on the strange metal door, they were surprised to see it open, and interior lights come on.

Of course, they entered and were amazed by the pictures.

One of the hikers, turned back to the door and called to the others.

"Look there, above the door, that must be the name of this place."

"Yes, I suppose so," replied one.

"I wonder what the name means?" said another.

"I know," shouted one, "I know the name. It's one of the tribes that located here, around Great Slave Lake. That was a long time ago. That was their name, the Dene."

"Hallelujah"

I was standing in an open field with my mother and father and a large group of strangers.

It was night. The distant city lights created just enough visibility that I could see them. So many people, children too, all looking up to the night sky.

It was the evening of the new moon and the stars shone brightly against the deep darkness. There was the Big Dipper, with its two stars on the end of the cup, pointing to the North Star. It was so clear tonight. We could even make out the Milky Way.

But what were we all doing here? What brought us to the open field on this night?

Some kids were in their pajamas, many without shoes. The adults next to us had thrown a blanket over their shoulders to brave the cool night air. Clearly, we all were in a hurry to get here. But why?

No one said anything. An uncomfortable silence hung over our group. The only sounds were from the wind whipping through the tall grass and the occasional late-night crickets.

I reached up and grabbed my mother's hand. I wasn't scared. I just wanted to feel her hand against mine. She looked down at me. She smiled, and without saying a word, looked back up to the night sky.

Suddenly there was a collective gasp from the crowd. My mother's hand tightened around mine. It almost hurt, but I didn't say anything or pull away. I looked up and let out a gasp as well.

From the vicinity of the Belt of Orion, it first appeared. A light ten times bigger than any star in the night sky. And it was getting larger by the second. It was moving towards us.

As the light drew closer, many dropped to their knees. I could hear soft prayers. Some were cheering. Some were laughing, a nervous laugh. But no one was crying. It was like they had expected this moment. Like they were embracing it.

Suddenly, my dad dropped to his knees. "Hallelujah," he said, "hallelujah."

Those were the first words he had said since we left our house. Before leaving, he shook my shoulders to wake me and said, "dress warm, son, it's going to be cold out there." That was all he said until "hallelujah."

As we walked from the house towards the open field, I wanted to ask what were we doing? And I wanted to know if I was dreaming. Again?

It was a long time ago. Ten years ago. But I remember that night so vividly. Was it really a dream? I wasn't sure, but my mother and father remained skeptical. At least they said they were.

Late at night, in bed, sound asleep.

My bedroom window looked out over the large open field.

Suddenly, a bright light woke me up. A large bright light. Round in shape. Just a soft humming sound. Drifting down on to the open field, pushing down the tall grass as it settled.

I cried out. My parents rushed into my room. "Are you alright? What's the matter?"

I looked out the window. But it was gone.

I told them exactly what I had seen. A large bright light landing in the open field behind our house.

My parents said it could have been the moon, but more likely a dream. "Yes. A dream," they replied. As hard as they tried to reassure me that everything was okay, it didn't work. I was convinced I had seen something in our backyard.

That was ten years ago.

Was it returning now? Amongst the crowd of strangers in the field behind our house? On this dark moonless night? Was the light returning?

"Hallelujah, hallelujah." My dad repeated over and over. My mom was still holding my hand, even more tightly now.

The couple next to us said something. "Isn't this wonderful? No one believed us, but we have been telling them for ten years that this day would come and here it is."

My mother turned to them and finally said something. "Yes, it's wonderful and all because of him." She was looking down at me when she said that. Straight down at me, with that big smile. She must have seen that I was scared now, probably could sense I wanted to run back to the house, to my bedroom, so her grip grew tighter. I wasn't going anywhere. I couldn't break free of her grip.

"Oh, it's him?" The couple was looking directly at me now. My dad continued his chanting.

My mother nodded in the affirmative.

"Thank you," they said in unison, kneeling before me. Then they turned and shouted, to the crowd, "it's him, he's here. He's here."

The crowd slowly turned in my direction. I could hear a rising chorus of "he's here, he's here." It grew louder and louder, until it was hurting my ears. Some reached out to touch me. Then it began, the entire field of people were looking at me and shouting hallelujah, over and over again. "Hallelujah."

Thinking back to that night ten years ago, after my parents told me to go back to sleep, that I was having a dream, a bad dream they said, they left me alone, once again, in my room. But I couldn't sleep. I went to my window and looked out at the open field. As I turned to go back to my bed, there was a gentle tapping on the window. I didn't see anything at first, but then they appeared.

As I edged closer to the window, I thought I must be dreaming. What were these strange creatures coming to my window? Then the one who was tapping, looked directly at me and said something. I didn't understand and raised my hands to tell it so. Aware of my confusion, the creature pushed a green button on his hand, and then I heard, "you are perfect. You will do."

Running to my bed, I cried out for my parents. Bolting back into my room, they again, told me I was having a bad dream and to go back to sleep.

"Hallelujah, hallelujah," the chanting grew more rhythmic now and louder. It was like the crowd had fallen into a deep trance. My mom knelt in front of me and said, "are you ready?"

"For what?" I screamed. I was scared, terrified. I started to shake. I wanted to run. To get away.

"For them," she said, "are you ready for them?"

That night ten years ago after seeing the creatures, I didn't go back to bed. I couldn't go back to sleep. I turned off the light on my bedstand and went slowly back to the window. There they were. My father and mother were outside, and … they were with the creatures. I pushed opened the window, just part way, so that I could hear them.

The creature spoke first. "We are here to complete our arrangement. Is everything ready?"

My mother was crying. Through her tears she managed to ask. "But why him, you still haven't told us why it is him."

The creature responded, "because he is perfect for what we need. Our analysis pointed to him, and only him."

Crying louder now, almost uncontrollably, she pushed for an answer. "There must be others who can help you. I don't understand why you want him."

The creature was unmoved. "It has already been settled. It's either him, or a war your people cannot win. You know that."

Father put his arm on my mother's shoulder. Was he explaining something to my mother? I moved my ear to the open window. "Honey, we agreed to this years ago. We can't back out now."

Sobbing, my mother replied, "I know we did, but it seems so unfair now. He's so young. Still so young."

The creature, now sounding slightly more sympathetic, offered the following. "But this is for the good of both of us. You will continue to occupy this world, and we can secure a new start with your son. Don't you see that."

She was looking for reassurance. "Promise me you won't hurt him?"

"Hurt him? Why would we do that? He will be our new Messiah and will help us overcome …". He didn't finish.

"Hallelujah, hallelujah." Suddenly the chanting from the crowd grew softer. The crowd rushed me again. "Don't touch him, you might bruise him." My father was holding up his hands. "It's part of our agreement. He must be perfect," my dad shouted. The crowd backed away.

The bright object was now directly above us. I could hear a slight humming noise. It was just like that noise ten years ago. The ground was vibrating as it slowly came to rest in the field. In the tall grass. It was directly in front of me.

The bright light dimmed. A door near the object's bottom slowly opened, revealing a room bathed in green light. So green, I thought. Stairs descended into the tall grass.

Back in my bedroom, ten years ago, hearing my mom repeat, almost begging, "promise me you won't hurt him. Please promise me," I slumped to the floor. Hurt me, why would the creatures hurt me?

As I crawled back to my bed, I called for my parents one last time. They entered the room. My mom's face was wet with tears. Explaining what I had just seen and heard, they shook their heads. "Tim, now you're definitely having a nightmare. Please come to bed with us. You will be fine in the morning. You will. You'll see."

That was ten years ago, I was only 6. I never spoke of it to anyone, not even to my best friends. At some point, I convinced myself it must have been a dream.

But tonight, in that open field, with the shouts of hallelujah filling the night air, it was all rushing back to me. The creatures, the conversations, all of it. Was it not a dream? A chill ran through my body.

The creature came closer. I recognized him. It was the creature who was tapping on my window ten years ago. "Is he ready?" it said, looking at my parents.

My parents nodded yes. The crowd's acknowledgement of their response resulted in a loud burst of "Yes, Hallelujah, he's ready."

One last hug from my parents, one last kiss on my forehead, as my mother slipped my hand into the creature's. Its hand was warm. My chill vanished as the creature's warmth spread through my body. For the first time, I wasn't scared. I looked up at it and said, "Yes, I'm ready."

I climbed the stairs and entered the bright green room. The group outside had fallen silent. I looked back. Some were walking away. My parents were waving, and my mom was crying.

The next morning, at least I think it was the next morning, I woke up in my own bed. I looked out the window, the crowd was gone.

Rubbing my eyes, I could see all my familiar pictures on the walls. My favorite of the full moon over the Pacific Ocean was there. My baseball bat and glove were where I had put them after yesterday's game. It was all there. I must have had a dream, all of it, a bad dream. I felt so relieved.

There was a gentle knock on my door. "Tim, are you awake, would you like breakfast? We are having your favorite, blueberry pancakes. Fresh blueberries from the garden."

Oh yes, the garden, where every year we would plant something new. It had been my turn to pick this spring, so I picked blueberries, my favorite. "Yes, I'm awake. Come in."

They came to my bedside. It was them, my parents. They looked so happy.

I guess it had been a dream after all, I thought. My dad looked at me, with a big smile on his face. Strange I thought, he hardly smiles, especially in the early morning before coffee. Mom looked down at me and said in her familiar reassuring, sweet voice, "After breakfast, we, well actually you, have a very important meeting."

Meeting, I thought? What meeting. There was no baseball practice today. No photography club meeting scheduled. "What meeting, dad," I asked.

"You will see. He's been waiting a long time to meet you. Ten years actually. He doesn't have much more time left, so today's meeting is very important."

"What are you taking about, dad?"

"You'll see son, now hurry up, I'm about to cook the pancakes. Blueberry, your favorite."

Both turned to leave, as they did my mom and dad gave each other a high five. Then I heard my dad say it. Whispering, perhaps he didn't want me to hear, but I did. He was smiling, mom was too. After he said it, he pushed a green button on his hand, and then I heard that too.

"Hallelujah," he said, followed by that strange language I couldn't understand ten years ago.

A Mouse in my House

"Don't rent. You're crazy renting."

Yes, I understood that, but I liked where I was. It was so convenient. And I had a great view of the park and the ocean.

"All that rent money you're wasting."

I guess I never cared about that. I just liked my small apartment."

"You could be building up equity in your own home."

But why did I need to do that? I was single, living alone. I really didn't need a home. The hell with building up equity.

"Besides, owning your own home is so rewarding. It becomes part of you."

But all that work. Mowing the lawn, raking leaves, shoveling snow, maintenance, replacing things. I shivered at the thought. Not sure I wanted any of that. Life was so simple now.

"And you won't have to sleep on the couch when we come to visit. And, with a spare bedroom we could visit more often and stay longer."

Well, that was the whole point, wasn't it? But of course, I couldn't tell them.

"And it will be great if you ever get married and start a family."

Oh, that again. Married. Children. They didn't understand. I was happy the way I was. A bachelor. Besides, my married sister had two kids, their grandchildren. Did they need more?

117

"Think of your future. Do you want to spend the rest of your life in this small apartment?"

I could see that actually. Even dying in this small apartment up on the fifth floor, perhaps looking out over the park and the ocean. One last, lovely view from my small fifth floor apartment before I closed my eyes for the last time.

"And how many times has your car been broken into because you have to park out on the street. Get yourself a house with a garage."

Well, that was kind of tempting. But, given that my rundown car was almost 20 years old and the only thing the kids that broke into it got were discarded McDonald's hamburger wrappers and yesterday's newspaper, why should I care. Yeah, I didn't care.

"And that old elevator. Out of order most of the time. Do you really like walking up five flights of stairs?"

Exercise, I thought. Given my desk job, this was the only opportunity for exercise. When the elevator was out of order.

"Besides, with all the development going on in your neighborhood, I wouldn't be surprised if the building is sold and converted into a shopping mall. Then what would you do?"

And so, it wouldn't stop. Finally, I gave into them and bought my own house. Two stories, two bedrooms, back yard, garage, and a mortgage. In the mountains, surrounded by tall trees. Away from the city. Isolated. Away from the park and the ocean. Away from that lovely view.

At first it wasn't bad, at least not as bad as I had anticipated. But then the leaves fell, and then the snow fell, and then it moved in.

It. The mouse.

"Probably trying to escape the cold and the snow," my neighbor, Jim, said.

"Never had this issue in my apartment."

"Well, welcome to the country."

"Any suggestions?"

"Sure, get a cat."

"What?"

"In fact, you can borrow ours for a few days. Puddles will take care of your mouse problem."

"Puddles?"

"That's what we call him. Funny, huh."

"I guess."

And so that evening Puddles took up residence at my house. I slept upstairs and Puddles was stationed downstairs.

The commotion woke me around 5. It was still dark outside. Downstairs, sounds of a battle going on. Puddles was hissing and screeching. Crashing noises. Then an ear splitting "rrrreeeeer," followed by silence.

Had the mouse been terminated? I made my way downstairs. The overhead light was on just as I had left it.

Entering the living room, I saw the evidence of the battle. The antique lamp was in pieces, scattered across the floor.

And there on the couch was Puddles. Shaking. Fear in his eyes.

Stepping towards the couch, I felt the dampness on my bare feet. Sticky too. Looking down, I realized why the name. Pools of urine littered the floor. Puddles, indeed.

Then, out of the corner of my eye, I saw it. The winner of the evening's battle. The mouse. The damn mouse.

That afternoon I dropped Puddles off on my way to the hardware store.

"Did Puddles solve your mouse problem?"

"Not really, but he did live up to his name."

"Huh?"

It was an old hardware store. I was the only customer. The owner greeted me with a look of suspicion.

"You new to these parts?"

"Well yes, I bought the house on the old mountain road."

He smiled. The look of suspicion drained from his wrinkled face.

"How can I help you?"

"I have a mouse in my house."

"You don't say."

"Uh-huh, a mouse."

"High tech or low tech?"

"What?"

"I can see this is your first mouse kill. From the big city?"

"Why, yes. The big city. Lived in an apartment. No mice. Just an occasional fly. That's all." Of course, that was a lie. But I certainly didn't want to tell him about those cockroaches. Well, at least I could step on those. But a mouse. No way.

"So, what's the low tech?"

"A wood-based wired snap trap."

"A what?"

"Here look."

He was holding up an odd-looking contraption. A small piece of wood with a network of metal wires on the top.

"The Victor M154 metal pedal mouse trap. The bait goes here, and when the mouse goes for it, snap, this bar comes down, and problem solved."

"Jesus, does it hurt?"

"If you get your finger in there when it snaps, it sure would. Happened to my brother once and you could hear him yelling all across town. His finger was never the same."

"No, no, I mean the mouse."

"Don't rightly know."

"How much?"

"One dollar, bait not included."

Later that afternoon I was sitting on the floor of my dining room, arming my Victor M154. The instructions suggested a small piece of cheese for bait. Cheddar or Swiss? I couldn't decide. So, I put both on.

Gently, ever so gently, I pulled the snap trap back into position, all the while thinking of the hardware owner's brother and the finger that was never the same.

I was sleeping so soundly when I heard it. A loud snap. Just one snap. Then silence. I smiled.

Hurrying downstairs, I rushed into the dining room. There it was, an overturned Victor M154. Under the dining room table, where I had placed it.

Never having seen a squashed mouse, I hesitated to reach for it.

But then I got up the courage. How bad could it be?

I quickly turned over the mouse trap.

"Yikes."

The mouse was not there. The cheese was missing too. How could that be?

The squeaky noise came from the other side of the room. I turned. Jesus, there he was. The mouse. And he was enjoying the cheddar, with the swiss next to him. I thought I saw a smile and thought I heard a chuckle. Jesus, really!

"How did it work? The Victor M154?"

"Didn't."

"Really, we'll that's a first."

"This damn mouse is a first."

"High tech?"

"Yes, the highest of the high."

"That'll be the Victor M260 Multi Kill Electronic Mouse Trap."

"Tell me about it."

"Kills mice with a high-voltage shock. No need for bait. Just plug it in, turn it on and wait. Light too, less than two pounds, excluding the mouse of course."

It was a big black box, like a plastic lunch box, with an entrance, just big enough for a mouse.

"This green LED lights up when a kill has occurred. Just open up this collection drawer on the bottom and dispose of the beast. Easy."

"I'll take it. How much?"

"129.95."

"Guaranteed to work?"

"No, but I've never had a dissatisfied customer, unless, of course, you ask the mice."

We both laughed. My mouse problem was certainly coming to an end.

It certainly was easy to set up. I plugged it in and cooked up my dinner.

I decided to celebrate with a big steak. Prematurely, I realized, but I didn't care. I was just going to sit back and wait for the green LED light to come on. No dissatisfied customers, I smiled, except, of course, for the mice.

The steak was over-cooked, chewy too. I should have gone out for dinner. Well, perhaps tomorrow, after the green light comes on.

The next morning, I woke to snow. About a foot, and still falling. I went downstairs and started a fire in the fireplace. Made coffee and then realized I hadn't checked out the electronic mouse trap.

Quiet as a mouse, I thought, the trap. Yes, that's appropriate. They should use that slogan in their ads. Perhaps I'll write them. Another satisfied customer.

The green LED light was on. Mission accomplished.

I lifted the box and reached for the handle to the collection box. Should be called the coffin, I chuckled, the coffin collection box. Yes, I'll include that in my letter.

The collection box slid open. I smiled. There he was. Looked like he was sound asleep. Yes, mission accomplished. I set the collection box down on the floor and reached for my coffee. I lifted my mug in celebration.

"Here's to the Victor M260. Worth every penny."

As I sipped my coffee, I glanced down at the limp body. Sleeping, he looks like he's had a nice long nap. Well, that's about to last forever. I laughed so hard, the coffee spilled out of the cup and on to the floor. Some into the coffin.

Then… Jesus, then he moved. He was moving. He was waking up. The collection box was his bed. Jesus. The mouse was alive.

He looked up, sat up, and jumped out of the collection box and ran into the other room. As he did, I threw my coffee cup at him, but of course, I missed. The couch, however, was now covered with coffee.

"That's it," I screamed, "I'm done playing games."

I followed the mouse into the other room. He was cornered. But I had nothing to strike him with. I grabbed the morning paper, the Sunday New York Times, and attempted to rolled it into a club. It was too thick. Papers went flying across the room.

"Damn those Sunday inserts," I screamed.

Inserts removed, I found myself with a decent size club. Surely, this will do the trick. But where the hell was that mouse?

Then I heard that familiar squeak. It came from the direction of the fireplace. There he was. In front of the screen, probably enjoying the warmth from the blazing fire. Probably mocking me, I thought. Jesus.

I lunged. The mouse ran between my legs. And I crashed into the fireplace screen, knocking it to one side.

As I turned, I saw the mouse scurrying up the stairs. Probably to my bedroom. Yes, that would be where he was heading. I ran after him and slammed the bedroom door shut.

Now I've trapped you, you little bastard. I'm calling a professional exterminator. Your days are numbered. I've won.

Slowing walking back down the stairs I could see the dancing shadows and the flickering light. Then I felt the heat and then I heard the roar. The fire had escaped the fireplace and was consuming the room. Spreading into the dining room.

I stood outside, watching the house burn. Jim came up beside me.

"Jesus, what happened?"

"The damn mouse, that's what happened."

We continued to watch as the second story collapsed in flame. The whole house was engulfed in flames.

In the distance I heard the oncoming fire engines.

I turned to Jim, "too late."

"Yes, but what about ..."

"The mouse in the house! He's a goner. Toast. Up in flames." I wanted to laugh, but then I heard it.

Turning around in the direction of the squeak, I saw him.

The mouse. Like us, watching the house burn to the ground. The damn mouse. He had won.

Sally

The view from the windows was amazing, and she never tired of it.

The blues and the greens were especially prominent today.

The swirling cloud formation suggested a large storm was gathering.

And eventually the lights, everywhere she looked. Little specks of light. Like sparkling diamonds.

To the east, it appeared, again.

A thin blue line ran across the horizon.

The blue line quickly expanded upward.

Suddenly the sky was ablaze with the glowing sun.

It was the 14th sunrise today. Only two more remained on day 90.

She was in the cupola. The International Space station's research module with its seven viewing windows.

The International Space Station, 250 miles above the surface of the Earth.

Directly below, the earth, like a giant blue marble.

"Hey Sally, how's the view?"

It was Bob, one of her fellow astronauts.

"Wonderful, as always," Sally replied, "I could sit here all day."

"Well, I wouldn't suggest that. It's your turn on the treadmill."

The damn treadmill thought Sally.

One of the studies assigned to the crew aboard the International Space

Station was aimed at investigating the biomechanics of treadmill exercise conditions during long duration space flight. Scientists were under the assumption that walking and running in microgravity would produce the same training effects as during normal gravity.

The astronauts on this mission were to test that assumption.

"Okay, on my way," Sally replied.

Before exiting the cupola, she quickly ran the numbers through her head.

Ten minutes to the exercise room, forty minutes on the machine, ten minutes for measurements, ten minutes recording results, and another ten minutes to return. Eighty minutes total.

"Ten minutes to spare," Sally said as she approached Bob.

"Huh?"

"I'll be back here ten minutes before the next sunrise."

As Sally started to leave Bob held out his arm, preventing her from passing.

"Sally, aren't you forgetting something?"

"What?"

"Our monthly broadcast?"

"Oh shit, is that tonight?"

"Yep, sure is. All of us have been asked to be in attendance too."

"My god, I wish we had been told about these damn broadcasts in advance," Sally replied. There was a definite tone of frustration in her voice. Anger too.

"Well, they thought the exposure would be good. You know, keep the public interested, keep the funding flowing."

"Fuck the public, fuck the funding," Sally replied. "All I get are the stupid questions. What's it like being the only female up there? Do you cook the dinner? Do the guys help with the cleaning?"

Bob didn't say anything, but he nodded in agreement. After a few seconds of silence, he spoke,

"Well maybe tonight they'll ask you who does the laundry?"

They looked at one another and then both broke out in laughter.

Glancing back at the earth, Sally mumbled, "well perhaps I can get back here for the last sunrise of the day."

The space station, traveling at a speed of five miles per second, circled the Earth every 90 minutes. As a result, the seven astronauts were witnesses to 16 sunsets and 16 sunrises within a 24-hour period.

The monthly broadcast began right on time. Tonight, they were connected to high schools on the east coast of the United States.

After introductions, a brief tour of the room from which they were broadcasting, and a few "tricks" from space — spinning a pencil was always a crowd pleaser — it was time for questions and answers.

"What does the earth look like from up there?"

"What is it like to sleep in zero gravity?"

"What happens if someone gets sick?"

And then finally, "Sally, do you do the dishes?"

Sally turned to Bob, smiled, then back to the camera.

"No, I stopped doing them two months ago. Now the dirty dishes are just piling up in the sink."

After the broadcast concluded, Sally hurried back to the cupola, but not in time for sunrise 16.

The observation room was full of sunlight.

"Shit," was all she could say.

"Hey, Sally, we're going to watch a movie tonight. Care to join us?" It was Bob. "Popcorn's on me."

"I don't think so, besides I'm tired of those damn war movies you guys watch."

"Oh."

"Yeah, let me know when you want to watch a chick flick?"

Bob turned to leave. As he did, he said, "actually the movies up here in the cupola are better."

"They sure are," Sally said.

"Good night, Sally, see you in the morning."

Sally said nothing, she just stared off to the west, waiting for sunset number 16.

At least I'll get to see that, she thought, even though sunrises were her favorite.

After sunset number 3, Sally's eyes began to close. The spinning earth beneath her was putting her to sleep.

She decided to strap herself in and sleep in the cupola. She had done that many times over the last three months.

At first it was a gentle shaking, a rocking motion, almost undetectable, but then it got more violent. And then there was one loud bang, like a pounding on metal followed by a pulsating grinding noise.

The space station was shaking violently, and it sounded like it was coming apart. Bursting at the seams.

That's when Sally woke up.

"What the hell?" she shouted, but of course, no one answered as the sleeping quarters were on the other side of the space station. Certainly, way out of voice range, even shouting range.

Sally unbuckled herself from the viewing chair and started to get up.

As she did the shaking became even more violent. Unable to walk, she held on to the back of the viewing chair and waited.

Slowly the shaking lessened. Eventually it stopped. The noise stopped too.

"Jesus Christ, what just happened?" was all she could mutter.

Just then, the station's alarms began to wail. The only other time she heard that ear piercing sound was when the system thought it detected an air leak. There wasn't one.

Sally made her way out of the cupola, and into the U.S. lab module. The plant experiments had come loose and were floating around the facility. Pushing her way through the clouds of dirt and vegetation, Sally exited the module into the long corridor leading to the other side of the space station where the living quarters were.

The space station, which was over 20 years old, had seen better days. Some of the insulation padding lining the walls of the long corridor were peeling away. Even graffiti had started to appear, with 'Leeroy Was Here', and 'For A Good Time Call' …

Sally knew it would take a good twenty minutes to get to the living quarters. After all, the space station was over a football field in length and as such was the largest man-made object put in space.

Suddenly it stopped. The alarm went silent.

"Thank God," Sally muttered although now the ringing in her ears took over.

Floating through the corridor, Sally realized that she had not had any voice communication from her six fellow astronauts. Strange, she thought, no way anyone could have slept through that commotion. But then, perhaps the communication network had been affected by the vibration.

Off to her side was the exercise module. The treadmill which had been bolted down had separated from the floor and was spinning like the pencil trick.

Well, that's a blessing, Sally thought, anticipating that the treadmill's demise would be the end of the Treadmill Kinematics experiment.

As she started chuckling about the condition of the dreaded treadmill, the lights in the corridor suddenly flickered, dimmed, and then went out. She was in total darkness.

"Shit, now what," she said, as she reached for her emergency flashlight.

But it didn't work. There was no light.

Then she realized that she hadn't recharged her flashlight after she used it two weeks ago while retrieving some supplies from the storage module.

As she threw her flashlight into the dark void, Sally screamed, "Jesus Christ, what the hell else can go wrong."

She had no idea at the time, but she was about to find out.

Slowly working her way down the dark corridor, in the direction of the living quarters, she felt what she thought was a breeze. Like something had rushed by her.

That's impossible, she thought, there are no breezes in the space station. There just can't be. I must be imagining.

But then she felt it again, but this time behind her,

"Who's there," she shouted, "damn it, is that you Bob?"

But, of course, there was no reply.

Reaching the entrance to the living quarters Sally was relieved to see that the lights in this section of the space station were still working.

The living quarters were a mess. The violent shaking had separated equipment from its bearings. Some food dispensers had sprung open and released their contents into the air.

But no one was in there.

They must still be in their sleeping quarters, Sally surmised.

The space station had seven small sleeping quarters, where sleeping bags were firmly attached to the walls. Nothing fancy, just a place to sleep.

The living quarters, and the attached command/communication facility, was the about the size of a six-bedroom house. Not only did it contain the sleeping quarters, but there were also two bathrooms, a full gym, an entertainment room, with a movie theater, a dining area, and a 360-degree view bay window.

"All that's missing is a bar," Bob would say. The other five guys agreed.

Sally would have preferred a beauty salon, but she didn't tell them.

"Is anyone here," Sally shouted. "Bob where are you?"

Again no one answered.

Sally was starting to feel uncomfortable. Uneasy actually.

A slight chill ran through her, something didn't feel right.

Then she felt it again. That slight breeze, just behind her.

"Hey guys, where the hell are you?"

Silence, followed by a slight echo of her voice. It was like she was alone on the space station.

Entering the command facility, Sally was alarmed to see it empty. One of the astronauts was to be there at all times and Bob usually had this time slot.

Yes, something's not right, she thought. Not right indeed.

Looking out of the bay window, she suddenly forgot the predicament she was in.

It was one of her favorite passes, coming up was the West Coast of the United States, then flying over the entire country, over the Atlantic, and then across Europe. All in 25 minutes. It was the one path that actually hit almost all the places she had lived. It was like a slideshow of her life.

The sun had just set to the west. Looking westward she could see the horizon of the Earth against the black background of space. Stars dotted the darkening sky. A lightning flash illuminated a large cloud mass over the Pacific Ocean just west of San Francisco.

San Francisco, where she interviewed with NASA. Where she interviewed after she decided she wanted to be an astronaut. Where they said yes, she qualified.

The lights of Las Vegas were next. Las Vegas, the city with the brightest night lights in North America. Nothing even close.

Las Vegas, where she went to college and where she learned to count cards.

"I was always good at math," she told the NASA team in the interview room. She smiled when she told them.

Next up, the lights of New York, the city where she was born. The city she could hardly wait to leave behind, and now the city which she missed every day.

Across the dark Atlantic, and then the lights of Paris. The city where she fell in love. Not just with the architecture or the food, but with Andre.

Andre wanted her to stay, to stay with him in Paris, but she was ready to leave.

Finally, he asked, "is it the sex? Is it not that good?"

She wanted to tell him it wasn't that good, but instead she told him she wanted to become an astronaut. She had to leave.

As the lights of Paris disappeared below the dark horizon to the west, Sally resumed her search for her fellow astronauts.

The sleeping quarters were just beyond the entertainment section. Bob's sleep station was first.

"Hey Bob, are you in there," she asked as she gently knocked on the metal door.

When there was no reply, she slowly turned the handle and opened the door.

Bob's sleep station, which was about the size of a large telephone booth, was dark.

Reaching for the light switch, she felt it again. That breeze, brushing up against her, like something exiting the sleep station.

The lights snapped on as she tapped the switch.

Bob was still in his sleeping bag. It was tethered vertically to the wall.

Sally could see that Bob was wearing his earplugs. No wonder he couldn't hear her.

"Bob, what the hell? Are you still sleeping?" Sally hollered.

There was no reply. Bob remained silent.

Sally moved closer, then she noticed it. Bob's eyes were wide open and his mouth too, like he had seen something. Like he had been screaming at something.

But he wasn't moving. He was frozen in place.

Reaching for him, her hand touched his face. It was ice cold. He wasn't breathing.

Sally slumped to the floor and let out a scream. Then she started sobbing.

After a few minutes, Sally visited the other five sleeping stations, where she found all five astronauts had suffered the same fate as Bob. They were all frozen. They were all dead.

Sally was the only one alive. At least for now.

Returning to the control room, Sally made her way to the communications console. Reaching for the switch, she hesitated. Something didn't seem right. She was suddenly overcome with impending doom, a consuming fear spread throughout her body.

As she fell back into the main control chair, she felt it. The breeze on the back of her neck. But this time, it wasn't fleeting. This time it stayed and grew stronger.

Her neck was getting cold, her body started trembling, she was shivering, uncontrollably.

Sally tried to speak, she wanted to scream, but she couldn't.

Something touched her. Definitely there was something touching her on her neck. She tried to turn but couldn't.

Then she felt it entering her body. Like a sharp knife penetrating her.

It was warm, it was almost comforting in contrast to the cold she had just experienced. Strange, she thought, why am I no longer afraid?

As her body warmed, she suddenly felt very hungry, like she hadn't eaten in days, perhaps longer.

How could I be so hungry at a time like this, she wondered.

Eventually, she fell into a deep sleep, but before she did the hunger passed.

At least she thought it did.

How long have I been sleeping? Sally wondered when she heard the call from NASA.

"Alpha Station, this is Houston, do you read? Please respond."

Sally reached for the communication switch, and struggling with the dryness in her mouth, spoke.

"Houston, Alpha Station here."

After the usual six second delay, Houston responded.

"Jesus, Alpha Station, what's going on up there. Are you okay?"

"Excuse me?" was all Sally could say.

"We've been worried sick about you guys."

"Oh?"

"Yes, Sally, we've been trying to reach you for a month. A whole month. What the hell is going on up there?"

"Houston, we've had an incident."

"Incident? What's going on Sally."

In a calm voice, which even surprised her, Sally related in detail what had happened.

After she finished, NASA responded.

"Information received, launching a rescue mission asap."

Two weeks later the space shuttle docked at the International Space Station. After entering through multiple air locks, the team reached the command facility. Sally was not there.

As the team open the closed sleeping quarters, they were stunned by what they saw. The six astronauts were no longer in their sleeping bags, but instead what remained of them was lying on the floor, their bodies in a decomposed state, almost unrecognizable.

Carefully, and without speaking, they returned each astronaut's body back into their sleeping bags and sealed each. When they finished, the team leader finally spoke,

"Well, this will be a mystery for Houston to solve. It's way above our pay grade."

Just then Sally entered the command facility.

"My God, Sally, are you okay? Where have you been?"

"Oh, I'm fine. I've been in the cupola."

"Well, let's get you back to earth."

At first Sally didn't reply, but simple stared at the six sealed sleeping bags, then she turned to the bay window.

"It's beautiful," she mumbled.

"Huh?"

"The earth. The view from up here is so beautiful. I could watch it all day."

The team leader turned to one of his assistants, shook his head and whispered, "she must be in shock, let's get her home."

After loading the six sleeping bags and Sally into the space shuttle, the crew returned to earth.

Sally was immediately put in quarantine for observation. After a week she was released and back at NASA.

The six astronauts were turned over to a team of doctors. Their results were expected within a couple of weeks.

However, at the end of two months the medical team finally met with the top NASA administrators. The lead doctor started the presentation regarding the deceased astronauts as follows.

"First we need to explain why our analysis took as long as it did."

He cleared his throat, perhaps stalling for time, perhaps trying to find the right words.

"To begin, the bodies were in such a decomposed state, so we needed to search for an appropriate method of analysis. Then when we got our first results, we could not believe what they were showing. Thus, we needed to start from the beginning, which we did numerous times when we kept getting the same results."

"The results," shouted one of the NASA administrators, "get to the results."

The doctor looked around the room, then back to his team that was seated behind him. Clearly, he was uncomfortable. Nervous too.

"Well… err … the six astronauts were … they were … consumed."

"Consumed? What the hell does that mean," a NASA spokesman shouted.

"Uh … they were … were eaten. Something ate them."

A collective gasp followed. Then the room fell silent. The NASA administrators looked at one another, then back to the lead doctor. One jumped to his feet.

"What exactly are you saying?"

"Something ate them. Right down to the bones. A few internal organs were not consumed, but very little remained. For the most part, they were picked clean."

"Jesus Christ, do you know what you're saying, what you're implying?"

The doctor shuffled his feet, and then replied,

"We're just presenting our findings. We're not implying anything. I suspect that's your job."

The meeting quickly broke up and three top NASA officials adjourned to another room.

After he closed and locked the office door, the Deputy Administrator spoke,

"What the hell was that all about? Do you really believe them?"

"Jesus, I don't know what to believe," the third in charge replied.

Finally, the NASA Administrator spoke,

"Gentlemen, we have a problem. I would suggest you sit down."

"Huh?"

"As you know, the seven-month mission to the planet Mars left one month ago. It is already 5 million miles from earth."

"Yes, and at our last meeting last week, it was noted everything was proceeding as scheduled. The spaceship was functioning as planned and the crew was fine."

As the administrator reached for the photo of the 7 members of Mars

Mission crew that he had placed on his desk just before the launch, he spoke,

"Well, that was a week ago."

"Huh!"

"It's been a week since we've heard from the crew. A God damn week."

"What?"

"A week ago, all communications ceased. The equipment did not indicate a problem. They just stopped communicating."

"Jesus, do we know what's happening."

The administrator continued to stare at the photograph. As he did, his eyes focused on the crew, then he spoke,

"I didn't have any idea, no clue, until a few minutes ago."

"What?"

The administrator's finger stopped over one of the crew members. Then he noticed the message the crew member had scribbled.

The words jumped out at him like a bolt of lightning. He felt like he was going to vomit. He read the two sentences out loud,

"Thanks for this opportunity to visit the red planet. It's like the ultimate feast."

He didn't have to look at the signature, but did, and very softly he said.

"Sally."

The Punishment

The wind was fierce and relentless. The snow was blowing sideways. The sound of my heavy breathing was accompanied by the sound of crunching snow with each step I took. Growing icicles dangled from my beard. And it was damn cold. Freezing.

In the storm I lost my sense of direction, even up from down. The snow was almost to my knees.

I could almost see the headlines about my demise. Former CEO Caught in a Fast Moving Blizzard. Well perhaps not, since I doubt anyone really cared now. Lucky if I would make it to the back page.

Not long ago, many would have cared. Many would have grieved. Yes, yes, I'm sure they would then. But not now.

I stumbled, face first into the heavy snow. As I did, my eyeglasses slipped from my face, buried somewhere.

Frantically, I pushed the wet snow from side to side. Moving quickly, paying little attention. Crunch. I heard the crunch. Jesus, in my rush to recover my glasses, I stepped on them. Holding up the twisted frames I could see that one of the lenses was cracked.

I had left in disgrace. Humiliation. From the company I had built from scratch. Into a Fortune 500 company in less than 10 years. Pharmaceuticals.

There were still a few hours before darkness set in. A few hours to find my way down this mountain to the safety of my car and out of this raging storm. But only if I wanted to.

Wall Street loved me. Shareholders too. Shit, I was even on the cover of Fortune, twice, and even nominated for Time's person of the year. They all loved me. Until they had reason not to.

So cold now. The temperature was dropping as the sun slid behind the cover of the horizon. Dropping in the winter sky like my reputation when the manipulation was finally uncovered. When the truth came out.

Angry now. Jesus, trying to see through this cracked lens is impossible. Removing the eyeglasses, I threw them as far as possible. Into the howling wind, into the blizzard, into the advancing darkness. Damn eyeglasses.

Manipulation was so easy. Too easy. We did our own drug trials and reported the results. It was only data, I argued. Arrange it so the results are what we want. What Wall Street wants. What our greedy shareholders want. Everyone will be happy. And they were. Until they weren't.

Why didn't I bring gloves? My hands were cramping from the cold. I wondered what the signs of frostbite were. Numbness probably. Well, I had that too.

We even manipulated the earnings we reported. That was easier than the drug trials. And the auditors didn't catch on. We had smarter accountants. Or at least more creative. Payoffs helped too. It was all part of the system, I told myself. Relax and enjoy the ride.

So reported earnings grew, all drug trials were positive. We became the go to company for business news, for the way to run a company. I was on Bloomberg at least one a week. It was so easy. It was so … deceitful.

The snow was become heavier now. I strained to move forward. Struggling to breath. Getting dizzy too. Should I stop here?

At first the new drugs produced little negative side effects. Some complained they were not getting better, but we responded that the drug was not 100 percent effective. That worked for a while.

Then, they started getting sick from the medication. Some were hospitalized. The medical profession was perplexed. The drugs which did so well in our reported trials were not working in their patients. An investigation was called for.

The snow was over my knees now. Each step was a struggle. My legs were aching. My face was numb from the bitter cold. I was gasping with each breath.

The baseball hat was doing little to shield my head from the bitter cold. Baseball hat? Who the hell wears a damn baseball hat in a snowstorm?

If only I had taken my cell phone, I could call for help. But I didn't bring it. I didn't want to.

The investigation uncovered our deception and a real audit of our financial statements revealed how we had misrepresented the company. The bottom fell out. The once darling of Wall Street became the devil. All that was wrong with the system.

I took my hat off and tossed it aside. The snow settled in my curly hair. I didn't even bother brushing it off. What's the use, I thought?

We went bankrupt. Millions of shareholders lost millions of dollars. Yes, we were the devil. And rightly so.

Then, the calls for punishment followed.

It was dark now. The snow whipped at my face. Each snowflake, like a sharp knife, inflicting pain on me. I stopped walking and just stood there with my eyes closed, absorbing the punishment, the pounding snow.

"You might get out in twenty years," my lawyer said after the guilty verdicts were handed down. By the tone in his voice, I felt he was hoping for more. A lot more. Perhaps he was an investor in the company. Jesus, had I screwed over my lawyer too?

My jacket was heavy and bulky. Heavier now with the wet snow. Pulling down the zipper revealed the thin shirt I was wearing. It was short sleeve too. More for mid-summer. But that's what I wanted. That's what I took from the closet.

I was told to report to prison in one week. My passport was seized. A monitor strapped on my ankle. One week to settle my affairs.

"You're lucky to get that," my lawyer said, "one week." He sounded annoyed, disappointed. Yes, he must have been a shareholder.

But I didn't know how to apologize. Perhaps this would be good enough for them. For angry Wall Street. For angry shareholders.

I tossed the jacket. My arms started shaking violently from the cold and the wind. Yes, this was more like it. Real punishment. But I was not finished.

"How could you?" my wife asked. "How could you do that?"

I had no answer. I wanted to blame the system, Wall Street, greedy investors, but I knew it was I who messed up. It was all on me.

"I don't know," I answered.

She shook her head, grabbed her two suitcases, and walked out the front door, to the waiting taxi. Our two kids by her side. None of them turned around. None of them said goodbye. Why should they, I thought. More punishment.

I decided to sit down. The snow was above my waist. I was shivering uncontrollably. Coughing too. My lungs were burning with pain. The snow continued. As did the wind. This was the punishment I sought. The punishment I deserved.

My eyes grew heavy.

As I felt myself falling backwards into the deep snow, I thought of it. Jesus, how ironic.

The drug we were working on before everything came to an end was for hypothermia and frostbite. But we probably would have faked those results too.

The Clever One

The parking lot was empty, except for one car in the employee parking area, but then it was only 7:00 in the morning.

I guided my Ford truck into the reserved spot. The black F150 came to a stop in front of the small sign. Reserved for Mrs. Smith. None of the other spots were reserved. I liked that.

Exiting the truck, I saw her at the front door.

Christ, she's always here before me. Always waiting for me to open. To unlock the front doors to the bank.

It was a small community state bank. Founded by my great grandfather, Earl Wells, just before the financial panic of 1889. Great timing, he told his family. But still he managed to keep the doors open throughout those terrible years and passed the bank down to his son. And then it went to my father, who unfortunately, only had two girls. And that where I entered the family line as the current president of the State Bank of Dodge Falls.

The 1889 financial panic started with a collapse of property prices. Eventually it spread to banks as home owners defaulted on their loans. My great grandfather kept the bank open by refusing to call in the loans of his neighbors. He was rewarded by that act of kindness after the panic as his neighbors came to assist him after the bank was robbed in 1895.

As the robbers drained all the cash from my great grandfather's bank, it was left insolvent. Rather than panicking with a run on the bank, his neighbors simply deposited more funds in the bank to keep it afloat. The bank was saved.

And so, the relationship between the community and the State Bank of Dodge Falls grew and flourished. And perhaps that was the reason why no other bank ever set up in the town.

"Couldn't compete," my grandfather said.

But of course, it was more than that. It was because of the special relationship.

"Good morning, Mrs. Smith."

It was Julie, one of our tellers. Young, shapely Julie. Blond hair, blue eyes. Every single man's dream, I thought. Probably some married ones too.

"You're here early, Julie." I replied.

"Well yes, Mrs. Smith. I needed to ask you a favor."

"And what might that be?"

"I have an appointment in the early afternoon, and I was wondering if I could have half the day off. Not sure how long it will last."

"That should be fine."

"Thanks, Mrs. Smith."

"Julie."

"Yes."

"I hope it's nothing serious."

"What?"

"Your reason for this appointment."

"Oh no, Mrs. Smith. Nothing serious."

I opened the bank door and followed Julie into the lobby. Quickly locking it after entering. The bank wouldn't open for another hour.

Tight clothing, I thought, how can she wear stuff like that? Like a spider attracting her prey. But, of course, it worked, didn't it.

As I walked across the marble floor towards my office, I glanced at the large rustic sign hanging over the tellers' cage. Proudly Servicing Dodge Falls Since 1888.

Well not quite, I thought. Not always serving Dodge Falls.

It was the best kept secret in Dodge Falls. Only the immediate family knew the real story that had been passed down generation to generation.

Each member sworn to secrecy. I made the mistake of telling my husband, Ray, and had him take the vow of secrecy immediately after I realized my mistake.

"Don't worry, honey, the family secret is safe with me. Absolutely safe," Ray assured me.

1895. The year of the secret.

My great grandfather came to the bank that day. Early as usual. As he sat at his desk, the telephone rang. He loved that telephone and prided himself on owning the very first one in Dodge Falls.

One year after Alexander Bell invented the telephone in 1878, my great grandfather had a telephone line installed from his residence to the bank. By the late 1880s, the novelty spread throughout Wisconsin. Dodge Falls was no exception.

Julie suddenly appeared at my office door.

"Should I open the front doors. It's 8 o'clock?"

"Err, yes," I said, handing her the keys. "I was daydreaming and didn't realize what time it was."

Hardly daydreaming, I thought. Day dreams are generally nice. Thinking of a loved one, planning a holiday. But not that phone call. That was not a daydream. I was thinking about that phone call over 100 years ago, when my great grandfather picked up the phone.

There was silence at on the other end of the line as he pressed the heavy headpiece to his ear.

"How can I help you?" He said in as cheerful voice as he could muster at 7 in the morning.

"Don't speak, just listen," was the reply.

"Excuse me?"

"I said just listen."

"We have your wife."

"What?"

"I said shut up and listen. We have your wife."

Kate, my great grandfather's wife. The love of his life. Some said Earl loved Kate as much as his bank. Others said the bank was a solid first.

$20,000. We want $20,000 by this evening, or you'll never see her again. Al least not alive."

My great grandfather was confused. He was not a rich man, and certainly didn't have $20,000 to give the kidnappers.

But my great grandfather was also a clever man, perhaps too clever. After all, how did he woo Kate to be his bride? Kate the most sought-after young girl in Dodge Falls. Too clever, his rival suitors contending for her hand all said.

After failing to negotiate the price for Kate's release, Earl proposed a plan.

The kidnappers were intrigued as he discussed his counter proposal for the release of his wife, and when they realized they would be pocketing more than $20,000, they quickly agreed to my great grandfather's plan.

They would rob the bank. That was the proposal.

"Just before closing, at 4, when the bank is less crowded and the days deposits are at their maximum, that's when you rob the bank," my great grandfather offered them.

"What about the guard? You must have a guard at the bank."

"Oh, sleepy Scott. Don't worry about him. I will distract him just before you enter the bank."

So, the time was set. 5 minutes before 4, today. The clever plan had been agreed to.

Throughout the morning and early after, my great grandfather checked his watch. He didn't even go out for lunch, and that was unusual for him. Lunch at the Dodge Falls Diner was a daily ritual. Liver and onions and black coffee. But not today.

The agreed time finally arrived, after what seemed like eternity for my great grandfather.

"Hey Scott, can you come into my office."

"Sure, Mr. Wells. Whatcha need?"

"I just wanted to talk, that's all."

As Scott settled into the chair across from the big desk, the front door swung open. They had arrived. There were four of them. All waving guns.

"Everyone on the floor. Do as we say, and no one will get hurt."

Scott looked like he wanted to leap into action, so my great grandfather whispered to him.

"Scott, it's not worth it. Do as they say."

"But … I…"

"No Scott, do nothing. It'll be fine."

Just then one of the kidnappers walked into the office.

"You too, both of you, out here, on the floor."

He didn't see Scott's gun, so my great grandfather gently nodded in that direction. The kidnapper noticed.

"Oh, and as for that gun. Let me remove that from you. No need for heroes, not today."

With Scott disarmed, the two of them were ushered into the lobby and forced to lie face down on the cold Italian marble floor.

"The safe, where is it and what's the combination."

My great grandfather had picked the right time for the robbery. The safe had been opened, ten minutes ago, as it always was, to move the day's deposits into the vault where it would be secure for the night.

"Over there," my great grandfather said, pointing to a concealed area behind the tellers' cages.

"And the combination?"

"No need, it's open."

Of course, it was, and the kidnappers knew it, but it was all part of my great grandfather's plan. Clever they told him when they agreed to the time for the heist.

With fifteen minutes the State Bank of Dodge Falls had been stripped of all its cash. By some accounts, $50,000.

My great grandfather waited by his office phone all evening. But no call came. He started to panic.

Perhaps Kate's home. Perhaps they tied her up and left her there. He was trying to convince himself that the human love of his life was alive and well.

Home he went. It was a short walk to the house. But it seemed like forever for my great grandfather.

Approaching the house, he saw that lights were on throughout the home. A comforting feeling washed over him. Surely, she must be there, he thought.

The front door was unlocked. They must have left in a hurry after they tied her up, he thought.

Rushing into the house, my great grandfather shouted her name, "Kate," over and over, "Kate."

But there was no response.

Rushing upstairs, "Kate, Kate." His anxious voice solicited no reply.

Desperate now, he ran into the bedroom. She must be in there. Tied up on the bed, he thought.

But she wasn't.

He slumped to the floor, and let out only a soft whisper, "Kate."

My great grandfather was confused, frustrated, seeking answers.

Then he turned towards her closet. It was open, and it was …. empty.

Kate was gone. It wasn't a kidnapping after all. She was the clever one.

I sat at my desk wondering how my great grandfather must have felt. The love of his life, leaving him like that. But how could he know? How could he know what she and her lover were planning.

But, of course, today it would be different. With private detectives to check up on one's spouse. One could see it unfolding.

I glanced up at the large clock on the wall. It was 2:30.

The phone rang. The call I had been waiting for. For weeks I had been waiting.

"Mrs. Smith," I said, "how can I help you?"

The voice at the other end was unknown to me. But of course, it had to be.

"We have your husband."

"Oh, really."

"Yes."

"So why are you calling me?"

"Just shut up and listen."

"Well, hurry up, I'm late for my lunch."

"Jesus Christ, lady, didn't you hear me, we have your husband."

"Yes, I heard you. So why are you calling?"

"$250,000. We want $250,000 if you want to see him again."

"Inflation," I said.

"What?"

"Inflation, compared to 1895."

"Lady, do you want to see you husband again, alive?"

I paused for a moment, I suppose for effect. I looked at the confidential report that had been delivered to me weeks earlier.

"So, what's it going to be Mrs. Smith."

"Oh that. Could you please tell Mr. Smith something for me?"

"Huh?"

"Tell him to go fuck himself. And tell him he can take Julie with him."

I hung up and rose to go for lunch. The Dodge Falls Diner. Liver and onions. Coffee too.

As I walked to the front door of the bank, I turned and looked again at the sign above the tellers' cage. I didn't mouth the written words, but instead thought to myself, so who's the clever one now?

A Second Chance

I was standing at the back of the line, about ten deep. Reading the fares for one way and round trips. Still not certain what I wanted to do, where I wanted to go, or even why I was here.

Everything was a mess of late.

Marriage ended in a bitter divorce. Losing my job at the lumber mill. Far too much drinking, too. My life had turned to shit.

The train station was very busy on this early Saturday morning. Families off on a weekend getaway. Smiling, happy families on exciting adventures.

And then there was me.

Said she had found her true soul mate. Jesus, what was that all about? What's a soul mate anyway, I asked her?

Twenty-five years at the local lumber mill, all for nothing, when the new owners decided to modernize. Downsized, I complained.

The young doctor looked at my test results. "Severe and irreversible liver damage."

The line was halved now, and I still didn't know what I wanted to do, where I wanted to go.

Soul mate. I told her I would try, even though I didn't know what that meant. "Too late," she said. And that was it. It was over.

"Why are you letting me go?" I asked the company foreman.

"Something about the budget and the company pension fund," he replied rather unconvincingly. Not sure he believed it either.

"Treatments? Is there something we can do?" I pleaded.

"Not really," the young doctor replied. He was shaking his head, "the damage has already been done."

Jesus Christ, my life was a damn mess, a God damn mess.

I was at the front of the line.

The clerk looked up and nodded. He didn't even smile.

Must hate his job, I thought. Well at least he has one.

"What do you want? Where are you going?" His grumpy voice confirmed it. He hated his job.

"Err, not sure. Any recommendations?"

"Recommendations? What the hell? Do you think I'm a travel agent?" His lips tightened. No, not happy at all.

"Sorry. I didn't mean to upset you." Jesus, there I was again. Always apologizing.

Like I did with my wife. Apologize for not being her soul mate. Many times over, but like she said, it was too late. Jesus after thirty years of marriage, it was too late.

"Come on buddy, there's people who know where they're going and want to buy tickets." It was the big guy right behind me. His wife and two young kids in tow. I wondered if he was her soul mate.

"Hey buddy, buy a damn ticket or get out of the line."

"I'm sorry," I replied. "I'm not certain where I want to go."

"Well, I can tell you exactly where to go," he shouted. His wife and kids were laughing. "Yeah, you tell him where to go, dad." His oldest kid was cheering him on, "tell him exactly where to go."

Must all be soul mates, I thought.

I turned to the clerk. He was frowning. He looked like he wanted to tell me where to go too.

And he did.

"Over there, in the far corner of the station. There's a window. It's closed, but just knock three times and tell them Alan sent you."

"What?"

"Over there. Three times. Alan." He was pointing at a small, closed window at the far end of the station.

I didn't move. There was nothing there but the closed window. No benches, no signs, no passengers.

"Really?" I finally said.

Just then the guy behind me poked me in the back.

"Jesus Christ, you heard him, over there." He was so close; I could feel his hot breath. Then both of his kids chimed in, "Jesus Christ, Jesus Christ." His wife broke out in laughter. Clearly it was fun for all of them.

Definitely a soul mate family, I thought, as I stepped out of line and headed to the closed window at the far end of the station.

It was a small wooden window. If you didn't look closely, you might think it was just a discoloration in the wall itself. No sign indicating what it was, or what was behind it.

Feeling quite foolish, I tapped on the window.

Nothing happened. I guess it was just a joke or a way of getting rid of me.

Then I remembered, knock three times.

The window slowly rose.

He was an old guy, dressed in ordinary street clothes. Chewing on the ragged end of an unlit cigar. Unshaven and very sleepy.

"Alan sent me."

"What took you so long?"

"Excuse me!"

"I almost feel asleep waiting."

"But how did you know?" I asked.

"Mind your own business about that. Here's your ticket."

The ticket had no destination printed on it, no price, just a track number, a seat number and a time.

"How much?" I asked reaching for my wallet, but he didn't answer.

"The train leaves in 10 minutes, so you better get hopping." The window slammed shut.

Track 100. That was odd as there were only two tracks at our small train station.

I knocked on the closed window again. Three times of course. The window opened.

"What the hell are you waiting for? The train leaves in minutes,"

"Track 100? Where is that?"

"Where it's always been. Just get out to the platform. Over there, use that door."

"But…" Before I could finish, the window slammed shut and I heard it lock.

I hurried to the door leading to the platform. Once outside I found I was alone. There were no other passengers and there was only one track. Track 100 right in front of me.

The train pulled into the station. It was a strange looking train, with just an engine and one passenger car.

The conductor stepped off the train, looked up and down the platform, and then blew his whistle.

"All aboard."

I stood there on the platform. Not sure what I was seeing. Not sure what to do. Then he looked at me.

"Best you get on board. We don't want to be late for our next stop."

Without saying a word, I climbed the stairs into the car.

"Welcome aboard."

"Thank you."

"Can I show you to your seat?"

I started to hand him my ticket, but he shook his head. "No need for that, you're in first class, seat number 1A."

"But?"

"No need for questions. We've been expecting you."

"Expecting me. But how?"

"Alan. He called us. Now, please follow me."

He led the way, to the front of the car.

"Here it is, seat number 1A."

"Uh."

"Is there a problem?"

"Well, I was wondering, where are the other passengers?"

"Oh, we'll be picking them up at the stations along the way."

The next station was about a half hour away. The passing countryside was not familiar. I tried to determine which direction we were traveling, but I couldn't.

Then the train stopped. The door opened and heard the conductor. "Welcome aboard ma'am."

She was an older woman, perhaps in her late 70s. Glasses and grey hair. She walked with a cane and had no luggage, not even a purse.

"First class, seat 1B" the conductor said as he showed her to her seat. The seat right next to me.

No one else boarded. We were the only two passengers on the train.

The train pushed forward. The countryside flew by, so did stations. We made no other stops.

I turned to the old lady. I felt I should say something. Start a conversation.

"On holiday?" I asked.

"In a way," she said, "you might call it that."

She smiled. I looked at her. There was something about those eyes, even behind her thick glasses. Something so familiar, so reassuring. So...

"And where are you going?" She asked.

"Don't rightly know. I guess wherever this train takes me."

"That's a good attitude," she said.

"Wine?" The conductor was holding two glasses.

"No thank you," I said.

"But it's included in the price of your ticket."

I wanted to tell him that I didn't pay for my ticket, but before I could the old lady gently grabbed my arm and said, "oh please do. You don't want an old lady to drink alone, do you?"

I wanted to tell her that I didn't drink, but looking into her eyes, I couldn't.

"Of course, I will join you."

We tapped glasses.

"To our journey," she said.

"Yes, to our journey."

The wine had a strange, but soothing, taste and an aroma I couldn't place.

Suddenly I felt sleepy. I closed my eyes and rested my head against the window.

The clatter of the wheels finally woke me.

"It must have been the wine," she said.

"Yes, it must have been." I turned in her direction. But it wasn't her, it wasn't the old lady. Instead, it was a much younger woman.

"I'm sorry," I said, "I thought you were someone else."

"Really? And who were you expecting?"

"The woman who was sitting here earlier. I didn't realize we had stopped."

She looked at me, with those eyes, those same eyes, but now without glasses, and almost in a whisper said, "perhaps it is me, perhaps we didn't stop."

The voice was the same, but her appearance had changed. No gray hair, no cane, no wrinkles. Now a young lady was sitting next to me.

I looked down; my legs were swinging at least 6 inches above the floor. My feet were no longer resting on the floor. And I was wearing kid's shoes. Buster Browns.

I reached for my face. The beard which I had when I boarded was gone. Instead, my skin was smooth like I hadn't even reached the age to shave.

My God, I thought, I must be dreaming. Or perhaps it's the wine. Why am I so much younger now? Yes, this had to be a dream, or the wine. The strange tasting wine.

I turned again to the young passenger next to me, but before I could say anything I felt myself dozing off again.

When I next awoke, I was in her arms. She was younger yet. She was holding me tight to her chest, and I was sucking warm milk from her breast. I tried to say something, but I couldn't. I didn't know how. I just made babbling sounds.

I looked up at her and suddenly I realized who she was. Those eyes, that smile, that voice. It was my mother. But how could that be? I hadn't seen her for over thirty years. Thirty years ago, when I left. Forever I told her.

She started singing. That song that I heard so many times, so long ago.

"Rock a bye baby in the treetop..."

I grew tired again, I was so content, so happy, being cuddled in the arms of my mother once more. As my eyes closed, I heard her voice, her sweet voice.

"Oh, my dear baby, get some sleep for your long journey ahead."

How long had I been sleeping; I had no idea? But the blast from the train's whistle woke me.

It was dark. Pitch black dark. I was submerged in warm liquid. Pushing out my small feet to free myself, I heard her voice,

"Oh, he's kicking. I can feel my baby kicking."

Then I realized what was happening. I was being given a second chance. A second chance at life.

Yes, this mysterious train was giving me a second chance. I closed my eyes and waited for my new life to begin.

Cyanocitta Cristata

Not sure how I noticed it. Just lucky, I guess.

It was lying off to the side of the narrow pathway. Almost hidden in the tall late spring grass. Limp and helpless, naked of feathers and half-closed eyes. A Nestling, I thought. Only a day or two old.

Struggling to get up, but too young to support itself on its undeveloped legs.

As I reached down, I heard the screeching above me, a loud, almost gull-like scream. It was coming from the tree.

The sun was in my eyes so I couldn't make out the actual source of the noise. But I knew it was a bird and I knew it was upset. Very upset.

Suddenly two large birds buzzed me, squawking their disapproval at my presence. As they circled, I was able to see them more clearly.

White faced with a distinctive bright blue crest, back, wings and tail.

Blue jays. Two of them.

Cyanocitta cristata, as my mother called them.

Looking back to the fallen bird, I immediately realized the circling blue jays were trying to protect it. Probably its parents.

Adult blue jays, their protective vigilance of their young, has given them the nickname of nature's helicopter parents. And rightly so, given that grey squirrels, crows, and snakes enjoy feasting on their eggs and newborns.

Human too are seen as a threat if they get too close. Many times, an adult blue jay will swoop down to beat an intruder's head with its wings, and sometimes plant a peck or scrape to the scalp.

My eyes returned to the fallen nestling. As it struggled in the grass, I knew what I had to do. What I must do.

Sprinting on the dirt path back to our home, I reached the front door. Our apartment was on the top floor, the second floor.

Two, three steps at a time, I dashed up the stairs. Gasping for breath, I rushed inside and into my bedroom.

The closet, I thought. Certainly, I could find something in there.

Tossing clothes and toys aside I found what I was looking for. An empty shoe box.

Perfect, I thought. This will be the perfect refuge.

Shoe box in hand, I ran back along the path to the fallen blue jay.

I fell to my knees and looked down.

There it was. So small. So helpless. So afraid. So vulnerable.

Setting the shoe box next to the nestling, I realized I would need to build a nest to place it in.

But what?

I looked around.

Grass might work, but I wasn't sure how to shape it into a nest that would last.

What to do? My mind was racing.

I was searching all around me when I thought of it.

Of course, the t-shirt I was wearing. It was old and soft.

My parents bought it for me when they went to the city without me.

I took it off and stuffed it in the shoe box.

Picking up the baby blue jay, I gently placed him in the cloth nest I had prepared. The I ♥ NY design provided an appropriate backdrop.

I certainly couldn't place the shoe box high in the tree, so I settled for two lower branches, which I could easily reach. I wedged the shoe box close to the truck, in between the two branches. It felt secure.

Now what about food?

Worms? Berries? Seeds? I had no idea, so decided to experiment through trial and error.

As it turned out, the baby blue jay ate all of them. But I wasn't sure if he really enjoyed what I was offering, or just too hungry to care.

The two large blue jays, who I now realized were the parents, watched my every move. I wanted to think that they knew I was trying to help. But in any event, they no longer squawked at me nor buzzed me as they had earlier.

For days, without exception, I visited the shoe box and tended to the baby blue jay.

Then, one night I awoke to the sound of thunder and pounding rain against my bedroom window.

Jesus, the shoe box had no cover. I envisioned the little blue jay trying to keep its small head above water.

Jumping out of bed, I dressed quickly, and then dashed out of the apartment with an umbrella in one hand and a flashlight in the other.

The trail was muddy. It must have been raining for quite some time. I wondered if it would be a rescue mission or a recovery mission. I shuttered at the thought. How could I be so careless not to put a cover on the shoe box at night? I felt a deep sense of guilt knowing what I might have done to that little blue jay.

Skidding to a halt in from of the tree, I was relieved to see that the shoe box was still lodged between the branches. But what would I find inside?

I pointed the flashlight into the shoe box.

The t-shirt was wet, soaking wet. The little blue jay was wet too. But he was okay. The branches from above had provided a natural umbrella.

And so, the next two weeks raced by.

Every day, I delivered food. He was definitely growing. Sitting up. Feathers were appearing.

Each time I arrived, the parents were perched above. Watching silently, probably on guard.

Everything was going fine, but then one day I oversleep. I stayed up to late listening to the Lone Ranger on our radio.

Picking up my morning dish of worms and berries, I made my way along the edge of the lake, along the beaten path to the tree. I stopped along the way to take in the view and thought of the upcoming fishing season. Hopefully the trout will be more plentiful this summer.

As I approached the tree, a sense of uneasiness fell over me. Something didn't seem right. Was it just a feeling.

Then I saw it. The shoe box was on the ground, my t-shirt off to the side.

A large cat was circling the box.

"Jesus," I shouted as I dropped the breakfast meal. "No, no, it can't be."

I bent down and looked in the box.

It was empty. Empty.

The cat came closer.

Picking up a stick I waved it furiously in its direction.

"Get out of here," I shouted.

It clearly wasn't intimidated. It moved closer.

"Inspecting the scene of the crime," I screamed. "Your crime?"

I picked up the empty shoe box and tossed it in the lake.

"Damn it, damn it."

I picked up a large rock.

"Damn it, you cat, damn it."

Just then I heard that familiar sound from above. The blue jays.

Looking upward I saw the two large jays, perched where they had been for weeks.

I wanted to tell them how sorry I was. That I had tried.

Then out of the corner of my vision it appeared. Not sure how I saw it. Just lucky, I guess.

I dropped the rock.

Just a small dot at first, getting larger and larger.

It arched down towards me and then up to the large branch, landing between his parents. The baby cyanocitta cristata.

I waved and turned.

As I headed home, I noticed a few trout jumping in the water.

I smiled and broke out into a run.

Well, it's going to be a great summer this year, I thought, better get the fishing gear ready.

The Phone Call

It startled me, the ringing phone at the side of my bed.

It was early in the morning. Probably my parents calling to wish me a happy birthday. February 27. Turning forty. But I hadn't slept well last night and didn't want to answer.

But it kept ringing.

Pulling the heavy pillow over my head didn't help.

It kept ringing. And ringing.

Reaching over to the phone, I lifted the handset and quickly placed it back down in its cradle. The ringing stopped.

But not for long.

Ri-i-in… ri-i-in… ri-i-in….

Knowing the piercing sound would go on forever, I gave in and answered.

"Hello." It was a voice I didn't recognize. Certainly not my parents.

"What do you want?" I tried to sound annoyed.

"Didn't you get my message?"

"Message? What are you talking about? How would I get a message?"

"On your phone, your answering machine."

"Listen, I don't know what the hell you're talking about. Answering machine. What the fuck is that?"

"Oh, I'm sorry. I didn't realize."

"Is this some joke?"

"No sir, it's no joke."

"Well, what the hell is your name?"

"Name?"

"Yes, what's your name. You called me. What's your name? I want to know."

He hesitated. Good, I caught him in a crank call. Now it was my turn to mess with him.

"I want to report you to the phone company. So, I need your name. And supervisor."

"Phone company? Supervisor? I don't understand."

"Jesus Christ, do you like waking people up and messing with them?"

"Oh, you were recharging. I'm sorry. I didn't realize."

"Recharging?" Now he had me confused.

"Yes, recharging."

"I was sleeping. Or at least trying to, until you called."

"Interesting."

I was growing tired of the conversation.

"I'm sorry, but I'm going to end this call. I need to get ready to go to work."

"Work? Are you still working?"

"Of course, I'm still working."

"What do you do? Work that is."

"I am a mailman; I deliver the mail. Door to door. On my feet all day."

"Outside."

"Jesus, of course outside. What would you think?"

"But the air? How is that possible?"

"What?"

"The air. The toxic air. How can you go out in it?"

"I don't understand. The air pollution's not that bad. Perhaps in Los Angeles, but not here in Colorado."

"Do you wear a special mask when you go outside, when you leave your bubble?"

"Mask, bubble. What the hell are you talking about?"

"And how do you protect yourself from the sun's deadly rays? A special suit?"

"Listen, I think this joke has gone on far too long. Do I get a prize for playing along?"

"Sorry?"

"A prize. You know, for falling for your act? Do I get a prize?"

"Well, I am prepared to offer you …"

"I knew it, I knew it. A damn joke. Am I on the radio now?"

"Radio?"

"Yes, the radio. What station am I on?"

"There is no station."

"Well, then what the hell is this? Why are you calling?"

"It seems like your warranty is about to expire and we'd like to offer you an upgrade."

"Warranty? What warranty? Certainly not my car. I just bought that three months ago."

"Car? You have a car?"

"Yes, I do."

"It must be an electric car then."

"What? Electric?"

"Yes, electric, or is it one of the new propulsion models?"

"I have no idea what you're talking about."

"How does it run? Your car?"

"Gasoline, of course."

"Gasoline? How do you get gasoline? We ran out decades ago."

"My '52 Buick. Runs on gasoline. The only thing electric is the radio."

"52?"

"Yes, my 1952 Buick. Bought this year. Brand new. Convertible too."

"1952?"

"Yes, Damn it. 1952."

"Oh, I am very sorry. I must have pulled up the wrong year."

"What? Wrong year?"

"Yes sir."

"How the hell do you pull up a year?"

"My mistake. I'm sorry."

"So what year are you calling from?"

"2252. February 27, 2252."

"2252. Are you shitting me?"

"No sir, sorry my mistake."

"I don't understand."

"A communication network error. Unfortunately, we've had a lot of them since you people killed off the planet. Again, I apologize. Have a good day.

Brothers

I could hear the ice starting to crack. First an almost unnoticeable soft groaning, then a louder grinding, and then an almost deafening crack. Like a giant whip snapping in the air. Crack.

Why the hell was I out here? In the middle of this frozen lake.

It was early spring, and all the signs stationed around the lake cautioned against going on the ice. Of course, I paid no attention to them. I guess wanted to be here in the middle of this frozen lake.

Even my dad told me, every spring.

"Springtime ice is never safe. It's old ice, riddled with thin spots that are hard to see. It's unpredictable. Never go out on springtime ice."

There was a second loud crack and then the ice surface fractured under my feet.

I slid quietly into the icy water. It was colder than I could ever have imagine. Soon I was in over my head.

Why hell did I venture out onto the springtime ice? It was probably the argument. I had to get away from him. But why here, in the middle of this frozen lake?

The argument with my older brother.

It seemed like we were always fighting about something. Today it was over our shared iPad.

I reached up, over my head, trying to find the opening in the ice. All I felt was solid ice.

The ice, I was under the ice. Above me a solid layer of ice.

Jesus, was I trapped under the ice?

The God damn argument. Over an iPad and a girl, this time. His girlfriend. Texting back and forth all morning. I just needed the damn tablet for a minute or so, probably much less.

"Come on, Doug. I just want to …"

"Sorry little guy, but this is far more important."

"But …"

"No buts little guy. iPad in use. You'll have to wait."

Little guy, that was his nickname for me when he wanted to get me going. Get me worked up.

And it always worked.

So, I did what I usually did, I threw my backpack at him.

As usual, I missed. The heavy backpack hit the wall. Loose plaster fell to the floor.

"Don't be such an ass," I screamed.

"Jesus, Tommy, I hope you're better passing a basketball. That wasn't even close."

He always had the better comeback. That made me mad too.

I could feel the heat draining from my body. The ice-cold water was sucking the warmth from me, from my fingers, legs, chest, face.

"Well, at least I scored in our last game, I shot back."

"Oh yeah, two points in a losing battle. What was that score again, LeBron?"

There he was again with the perfect comeback. Would I ever top him? Shit, no way I thought.

Well, we did lose, and the game wasn't even close. When it was garbage time for the other team, the coach put me in. Less than two minutes to go, and I heard him shout, "Tommy, get in there."

Not even sure how I scored that basket. I think my eyes were closed. Just threw it up, it rolled around the ring, and slowly dropped through the basket just as the buzzer sounded ending the game.

Shivering now, face numb, I wondered if the final buzzer was about to sound for me. Probably wouldn't hear it down here, under the frozen ceiling above me.

"And by the way, little guy, wasn't that your first points of the season?"

Christ there he goes again. I hated him. Hated him. Suddenly I wished it was him under the ice. Thrashing his arms and legs under the thick ice. Feeling his whole-body numbing. Fearing the final buzzer.

Damn it, why couldn't it be him.

And he was right; those were my first points. How ironic, I thought, probably my first and last points I'll ever score in a basketball game.

Last, Jesus, I was always last when it came to the two of us.

Last to get dessert at the dinner table, last to call passenger "shotgun" side when getting in the car, last one to get his hand-me-down shirts, last to ….

Damn it, it should be him under the ice. Freezing under the ice. It should be him.

The ice above me was in shadows. The tall trees that surrounded the lake were casting their long shadows, like giant arms, giant hands across the icy surface. How I wished they could pull me from the frigid waters. Those giant hands.

"And by the way, little bro, your hands are too small to play basketball."

"No, they're not."

"Hold them up to mine. See what real basketball hands look like."

"No way, Doug, not falling for that trick again."

"Oh, come on, for real this time. No tricks, I promise."

I hesitated, remembering the last time he suggested we compare hand sizes, he squeezed my hand until it turned white.

Slowly I put my hand against his, still not quite trusting him.

It was much bigger. His hand was much bigger than mine.

"See, little guy. Your hands are too small."

And they were small. But then he was first string on the high school varsity basketball team; I was only second string on the junior varsity. He was the star of the team, and like the sun, everything, everyone revolved around him, especially girls. Jesus. I was just a little nondescript comet,

167

drifting aimlessly through space, not even observable with the most powerful telescope.

And now I was here, under the ice. That small comet, that no one could see, that no one wanted to see, because they were all so in love with the brightest star in the sky, Doug.

Yeah, he should be under the ice. Not me. Doug should be under this damn ice.

The shadows were gone. The arms and hands had retreated back to their respective trees. They would be no help now.

I remember the first time my big brother put his arms around me. I had fallen off my new bike. My first bike. I was crying. He reached down and helped me to my feet. My knees were scraped and bleeding.

"Don't cry Tommy. It'll be okay. Everyone falls when they're learning."

"Did you?" He was wiping the tears from my eyes.

"More times than I could count."

I was still crying when he put his arms around me.

"Don't worry, little brother. I'm here. I'll always be here for you."

Thinking back to that time, I suddenly realized that I loved my big brother. And I realized he loved me too. Always, we would love one another. We were brothers.

Right then, if I could cry underwater, I probably would. Tears too would drift through the icy water. But I couldn't. It was too cold. I wanted to cry, but I couldn't.

Oh God, it would be him, my big brother. It was him that I would miss the most.

Icy water was filling my mouth, reaching up into my nose. My ears were ringing.

I was numb all over. My heavy wet clothing was dragging me down. To the bottom of the lake. That's where they'd find me.

Then,

A loud cracking noise. Many of them, from just above me.

My hands were being pulled up; I was being lifted from the icy water.

I couldn't open my eyes. They were stinging from the cold water.

I was shaking, violently. Something was pulling me, across the ice, across the rough surface of the ice.

Suddenly there was hard ground beneath me.

I was pulled to a standing position. Where was I? Had I drowned?

Then I heard that familiar voice,

"Jesus, little bro, what were you thinking?" It was Doug. "Thank God, I saw you from the bedroom window. Saw you fall through the ice."

"I was ..." I couldn't finish, I was too cold to speak.

"Jesus, little bro, I'm glad I saw you. I don't want to think what might have happened if I hadn't."

I slowly opened my eyes. He was standing there, in just a t-shirt and jeans. Not even wearing shoes.

I started crying.

He put his arms around me and pulled me close.

"Don't cry Tommy, I'm here. I'll always be here for you, after all, I'm your big brother."

Opportunity Cost

"Can anyone explain the concept of opportunity cost?"

It was my beginning course in economics at the university. An early morning class too.

"Anyone?" The professor asked again, taking a sip of his morning coffee.

He almost fell out of his chair. Alan, my boyfriend. He had fallen asleep 10 minutes into this morning's lecture. "So exciting, macroeconomics," he said, just as he dozed off. Actually, he was usually out after five minutes, so this morning was a new record for him staying awake.

"Something about choices," a voice from the back of the room broke the silence.

Alan grunted. He was awake now but not sure where he was.

"Welcome back," I whispered.

"What?" He shook his head and yawned. "Is class over?"

"Hardy, another 45 minutes to go."

"Jesus, I hate these Tuesday Thursday classes. Too damn long."

"Okay, let's think about that. Something to do with choices." Professor Gordon said.

Professor Gordon was new to the university. His first semester teaching. From California, we all thought. Perhaps it was the deck shoes. He always wore them. And no socks too. Some lectures I would just stare at those

171

bare ankles. "At least it was better than the tedious lecture on GDP, I told my roommate.

"Choices. How do we make a decision regarding choices?" Professor Gordon asked.

"I could care less," Alan whispered. He was wide awake now.

I thought about it. Choices. This morning in the cafeteria, I could either have eggs, or pancakes for breakfast. I selected the eggs. Why? Easy, I don't like pancakes. Could the answer be that simple? What I like and what I don't like?

I raised my hand.

"Yes, Miss Jones, what do you think?" He moved closer to where I was sitting. I could smell his coffee and his aftershave. Strange combination, I thought.

"Comparing, something you like against something you don't like."

He smiled. Oh goodness, he smiled, did I answer correctly?

"Can you give us an example, Miss Jones?"

I sure can, I thought. I explained to the class the choice I made at breakfast. That should do it.

"How stupid," Alan said almost under his breath. 'What a dumb example." He was laughing now.

"But what if it was it between eggs, Miss Jones?"

"Excuse me?"

"It seems like you enjoy eggs. Is that correct?"

"Well, yes."

"Prepared anyway? The eggs."

"Except for soft boiled."

"So, what if your choice was between scrambled and fried?"

He was smiling and waiting. Waiting for my answer. I was shifting nervously in my chair now. Jesus, why did I try to answer his dumb question in the first place.

Alan was tapping his pencil on his desk. God, that was annoying. He knew it bothered me, yet he still did it. I wanted to grab the pencil out of his hand and throw it across the room.

"I don't know, Professor. Perhaps whatever appealed to me?"

"And why would one appeal to you more than the other?"

Jesus Christ, I wanted to scream, how the fuck would I know. But instead, I replied, "good question, sorry I have no answer."

"Teacher's pet, didn't know the answer." Alan was smirking now. He slapped his knee.

We had been dating for about a year now. We met during our first semester and were almost immediately attracted to one another. My girlfriends said it was a match made in heaven. Lately, I thought more like hell.

"No, no, Miss Jones. Think it through. You're going down the right path. Just think."

Alan was so nice at first. So thoughtful. Never criticized me. Nothing but compliments. Even bought me flowers on occasion. And it was fun to be with him. A perfect couple, his friends would say.

"Perhaps it's a visual thing? What looks good, or better than the other."

Alan was good looking too, I recalled. That blond curly hair was a turn on and at six two he was an imposing figure. I definitely liked the way people looked at us when we walked into a room. At least, I used to.

"Okay, Miss Jones, now we're getting somewhere."

But then something happened. Alan was like a different person lately from the one I first met that night at the basketball game. He went from a nice guy to mean. First verbally, but lately physically.

Alan slipped a piece of paper over to me. It read, Miss Jones, don't you want to get somewhere with me? P. Gordon. Jesus Alan. Sometimes I could just scream and other times I could cry.

"Miss Jones, consider making a choice between doing two things. Assume you want to buy a new dress, but you can only pay for it by taking money out of your savings account. How would you analyze that choice?"

Alan smirked. "No need to choose. Daddy will pay for it, or maybe some other cool guy in your dorm."

Jesus, he was really going on this morning. Just a continuation of last night. Last night he was over the top. He even slapped me. And last night was the first time I thought about leaving. But I didn't.

I wanted to say something to Alan, but Professor Gordon was waiting for my reply.

"I guess it might depend on how much money I was earning on my savings in the bank. The ..." I couldn't think of the word.

"Interest rate, Miss Jones. Excellent, what you would have given up, the lost interest, would be the opportunity cost of acquiring that dress."

Alan leaned over, "Excellent, Miss Jones, excellent, just like in bed."

In bed, that too. Wonderful at first, but lately he was aggressive, too aggressive. I told him he was hurting me, but he did so anyway. He actually seemed to like hurting me. I didn't understand why.

"But, Miss Jones, we can't always measure the opportunity cost in terms of lost income. Sometimes, as you suggested, it involves relative feelings. Similar to the concept of marginal utility, perhaps. How much extra enjoyment do you gain, selecting one over the other."

Alan jumped in. He was almost shouting. "Feelings, Jesus Christ, now we're talking feelings. I thought this was economics." Alan was laughing now. He didn't care that those around him heard him, even Professor Gordon.

"Alan, do you think this is funny?" Gordon was standing over Alan's desk now.

"I guess I do. Actually, I do. Feelings, how do you measure feelings?"

The whole class went silent, even Professor Gordon.

Then, he started to speak.

"Perhaps we should ask Miss Jones, how she measures her feelings." Professor Gordon was looking right at Alan and then he turned to me and back to Alan.

"Miss Jones."

It was then, that very moment, that I understood and appreciated the concept of opportunity cost. It was then that I realized giving up Alan would have a positive effect on me. The cost of holding on to him was far too great.

I got up and turned to Alan.

"Alan, the cost of my relationship with you is far too negative. It's like a minus interest rate. I'm losing money. I'm losing feelings staying with you.

My positive feelings are fading. It's time to make a choice, and I choose to say goodbye."

I started to walk to the back of the room, to the exit. Everyone, except for Alan stood and cheered. Professor Gordon just smiled.

I still wonder to this day, if Alan really understood the concept of opportunity cost, and what he lost by mistreating me. But then I guess it didn't really matter, because at least I understood what I had gained.

Zippy the Clown

The party was set to begin at 4. Everything was ready. The cakes, the balloons, the plastic swimming pool was full. Even the visit from Zippy the Clown had been confirmed.

The ad in the paper promised a day you'd never forget. Zippy the Clown, only $200 for the afternoon. He'll leave you in stitches the ad promised.

"Do you think we should?" She asked.

"What?"

"Have Zippy," she was laughing.

"Why not, he looks like a nice chap." I was laughing too. "And that's quite an outfit."

"And he juggles, too."

"Just what does he juggle?"

"Well, the brochure says anything from small children to knives." She was looking at the brochure that Zippy Company had sent us. And laughing again.

"Really? I need to see that. Small children, you said." I could hardly contain myself. I was tearing up as I laughed.

The kids and their parents started arriving at a quarter of four. Eventually ten kids and 20 parents would be wandering around our back yard.

"Do you think we have enough cake?" I asked.

"More than enough." She replied pointing at the picnic table with the four large cakes. "You'll probably be eating cake for a week."

"With ice cream, I hope."

She avoided answering me, but instead pointed at my belly.

"I know, I know," I said.

Ever since the Covid pandemic, I had lacked the motivation to exercise. And now, even with restrictions lifted, I still couldn't find the energy to go to the gym. "I had fallen into the no-exercise comfort zone," I told her. "What's that got to do with ice cream?" She would occasionally ask.

It was Henry's birthday, and since the pandemic forced us to cancel his party last year, this year we were going all out. Zippy was part of that. He'd keep us in stitches, and after all, that's certainly what we needed after a year and a half of the pandemic. In stitches, just as the brochure promised.

"Anyone missing?" I asked.

"Everyone's here except for the Zip," she said.

"Probably going to make some grand entrance," I replied. "With his knives."

"And little children?" She smiled.

"No need, plenty of them here."

The backyard was alive with kids. After all these months, it was a joy to watch. Pool water was going everywhere. Some helium balloons were trapped in the trees.

"Great birthday party," Alice said. She was my wife's best friend. Her son, Joe, and our son were best friends too.

"Just wait." I said.

"Wait. For what?"

"The main attraction. Zippy the Clown." I handed her the brochure. "Guaranteed to put us in stitches," I pointed at the large print under the picture of Zippy.

"I'm looking forward to that. Does Henry know?"

"No, we want him to be surprised."

The cake was ready to be cut. Two candles on each of the four cakes.

"He's turning eight," she said. "Two times four."

The cake was distributed. Not much left for the rest of the week, I thought.

We broke out into song.

"Happy birthday, to you …"

Suddenly there was commotion at the front door. The doorbell was in a constant state of ringing. The dog was barking too.

"I wonder," I said, going around the side of the house to the front. "Is it him, at last?"

There he was, in full costume. Those oversized shoes, baggy pants, colorful shirt, bright white face, big red nose, and floppy hat. Zippy the Clown, with his hand pressed against the doorbell.

"You must be Zippy," I said.

"But of course, I am. Were you expecting someone else?" He tossed his floppy hat in the air.

Strange, I thought, why would he ask me that? Perhaps it's part of his clown routine.

"No, no, of course not."

Taking a deep bow, he replied, "Zippy, at your service. At your disposal. Here to please. To tickle your funny bone, to …"

I stopped him mid-sentence, "and to put us in stitches."

He smiled, a kind of odd smile, I thought, and then he continued, "but of course, to put you all in stitches."

As I started to walk to the back, I responded, "Please follow me Zippy." But then I turned and faced him. "I feel weird calling you Zippy, calling an adult, Zippy. What is your real name?"

"Real name." He raised his voice. "My real name?"

"Yes, what can I call you. Your real name."

His voice softened. "My real name is Zippy. Zippy the Clown."

Okay, I thought. I'll go along with this guy's game.

"Alright Zippy everyone's in the backyard."

"Are you sure? Are you sure everyone's here?"

Jesus, why would he ask that? I was starting to wish I never saw that ad.

"Yes, the party started about an hour ago. We've had cake and did the usual birthday song."

"Perfect then. There will be no distractions for my performance."

"Yes, I think that's what you can expect."

Zippy turned to me and came close, "and you?"

"Me what?"

He was grinning now; his big red nose was almost touching my nose. I could feel his hot breath on my face.

"What do you expect?" he said.

"What?"

"I'm sure you have some expectations. So, what were you expecting me to do here? What were you expecting from Zippy the Clown?"

"I guess just the regular clown stuff. Acting silly. Making the kids laugh."

"Laugh, why do you think they'll laugh?" His voice rose again. He seemed agitated.

"Well, isn't that what clowns are supposed to do? Make people laugh." I felt my stomach knotting up. Jesus, what's going on here.

"Do you know that most kids are afraid of clowns? Kids actually fear us. Did you know that?"

"Well, no, I didn't."

"How can we make kids laugh, if we frighten them?"

"Sorry, I didn't realize."

"And then there's the dark side of clowning," his voice lowered. Almost whispering.

"Dark side, what dark side?" I asked, wishing this conversation would end and Zippy would leave.

"John Wayne Gacy."

"Sorry, the name means nothing to me."

"Then how about Pogo? That was his clown name. Pogo the Clown."

"No, still no connection."

"Pogo the clown. Assaulted and killed 35 young men in the Chicago area in the 1970s. And you know what he said when they caught him?"

"No idea."

"He said, clowns can get away with murder."

"Why are you telling me this?" I asked.

"Just thought you'd like to know before I put you in stitches, that's all."

He suddenly lunged for the picnic table. Pushing aside the remaining cake he grabbed the large cutting knife. He was laughing now. A very loud laugh. Everyone in the back yard turned in his direction.

"Hello everyone, I'm Zippy the Clown, and I'm here to entertain you. Well not really entertain you, but simply to put you in stitches."

He jumped from the deck to the backyard. Holding the large knife above his head, he shouted "who wants to be first."

Kids were screaming, parents too. There was nowhere to hide, with the back yard fully enclosed. He jumped into the plastic pool.

"Come on, you'll all have a turn, but who wants to be first," Water was splashing everywhere.

"Me," I said. "I'll be first." I was standing just behind him. I had grabbed another knife from the picnic table.

As he came at me, I heard the sound of the police sirens. They were stopping in front of our house. A fire engine and an ambulance, too. They were all here.

The knife went into my side. Sliding in, I felt a searing pain. I fell back. The knife still in my side.

The police grabbed Zippy. His arms were flailing. They pinned him to the ground.

"Damn, how does this guy keep escaping?" One officer said. "I thought the psycho ward had good security."

"Beats me." Another replied. "A clown thing I guess."

The medic bent down at looked at the knife in my side. "That's gotta hurt," she said.

"Hell of a way to ruin a birthday party," I replied.

"Sure is," she said, "and your wound is going to require a hell of a lot of stitches."

Looking up at her, I replied, "I wouldn't have it any other way, after all that's what the brochure said."

The Cuckoo Wasp

"How long has this been going on?" He was looking at my right foot.

"A couple of weeks, or so."

"This is very strange. I've never seen anything like it."

Hardly a reassuring response from my doctor, I thought.

"I think we should take a sample and have the experts look at it."

Experts, why do they refer a situation to the experts when they don't have an answer? Didn't they all go to medical school and learn the same stuff?

"Okay, that makes sense to me."

Doctor Kelly removed the knife from its sterile wrapping.

"Hopefully this won't hurt much."

What difference does it make, I thought? I'm the one getting scraped. Just do it. Get on with it.

When it first appeared, I was still able to put my shoe on, but after a week, I couldn't. No way I could get my shoe on my right foot now. Not even a sandal. As it was, I had to come to his office with my right foot wrapped in a towel. "A bad infection," I told the surprised patients in the waiting room. In spite of my explanation, two got up and quickly left. As they looked at me, I could tell that it was the smell that drove them away. That awful smell from my towel wrapped right foot.

"You ready?"

"Sure, do it."

I felt the knife against my right foot. There was no pain. None whatsoever.

"That's strange," Doctor Kelly said, holding up the knife.

"What's strange?"

"The knife, it wouldn't cut into the … the."

The what? I thought. I guess there is no name for what was now covering my right foot. From my toes to just above the ankle. My foot was encased in that material, that shinny blue, scaly, stinking material.

"Look," he said showing me the bent blade.

"Jesus, that's crazy."

"Let me try something else," he said as he left the examination room. "I'll be right back."

Probably needed to get away from the smell, I thought. Strange, how I've gotten used to it. After the first couple of days, I hardly noticed the smell. In fact, at times, I found it quite pleasant. Yes, that was strange.

"Ok, let's try this." He was holding one of those circular saws that doctors use to take off a cast.

The saw started spinning. He pressed it against the blue, scaly covering. Spinning faster now. Faster. Faster. Then it started smoking and the motor sputtered to a stop.

The saw's edge was chipped. Pieces had fallen to the floor. But the material encasing my foot was unaffected.

My doctor said nothing. He was looking at his broken saw and shaking his head. He started to speak, but nothing came out. He was out of ideas and out of words.

"Where do we go from here?" I broke the awkward silence.

"Uh, not sure."

"Who should see me now?"

"I have no idea."

Experts, I thought. Where are all those damn experts now?

"Why don't you go home and let me make some phone calls. I will get back to you tomorrow."

As I hobbled out of the examination room, I could hear my doctor talking to his nurses. "Jesus, did you see that, did you smell that? Whatever you do, don't let him back in this office."

And so it began, first, rejection from my doctor, then, rejection from my friends. Certainly, I couldn't go back to work.

"I need to take some time off."

"How much time?" my supervisor asked.

"I'm not sure."

"Well then don't bother coming back."

Eventually, I had meals delivered to my front door. I never opened the door until I was sure they had left. Then one day, when I did open the front door, they saw me.

The kids in the neighborhood, who I use to go fishing with on weekends, whose baseball team I had coached to the city championship, who I had set off fireworks with last July, they saw me reaching for the delivery at my front door.

They screamed. And then they ran. They didn't look back. And they never came back.

Who could blame them? In the month since my doctor told me to go home, the blue scale had covered my face. Not my mouth, nor my eyes. But I now looked like a ... monster, I told myself when I looked in the mirror. No wonder they screamed. I did the first time I saw my face, or whatever that was, staring back at me. After that day I removed all the mirrors.

As the weeks rolled by, the changes accelerated. My entire body was now covered with the shiny blue scales, like protective armor. My two legs had shriveled to six smaller legs. My hair was replaced by two horn like appendages. And two sets of wings had sprouted from my back. My face was dominated by a large, mouth-like chewing apparatus. Finally, my size. I was no longer six foot, but had shrunk to about half an inch.

Jesus, I somehow had become an arthropod, a wasp, a cuckoo wasp. That was the only explanation.

Yes, it must have been that hike with John. We were collecting insects for the entomology department at the University. John was a professor in the "bug" department, as I liked to call it.

"They're insects, Charlie. How many times do I have to tell you? Insects, not bugs."

Insects, bugs? Why should I know the difference? I was a young professor in the Econ department. What the hell did we know of bugs, or insects?

"Well, they're all bugs to me, John."

The morning was uneventful, at first. A few checkered beetles, one tarantula, two monarch butterflies, and at least a dozen lady bugs.

"Hey, John, how come these are called lady bugs and not lady insects?"

He just looked at me. And rolled his eyes. I knew he wouldn't be answering.

Then he saw it, the rare cuckoo wasp, sometimes called an emerald wasp, because of its brilliant metallic color, blue. They generally fly only during the hottest and driest months of the summer, and they generally fly alone. And here was one, circling around us.

John was beyond excited. This was his first cuckoo wasp. I just wanted to stop for lunch.

Waving his butterfly net in the air, John desperately tried to snag the cuckoo wasp. He missed.

The cuckoo wasp was clearly upset. His buzzing grew louder. He rose in the air above John's outstretched net. Circled. Then dove at us. I covered my face. Then the cuckoo wasp buried his stinger in the back of my neck.

Having won the battle, the cuckoo wasp flew away. My neck was burning.

"You should see a doctor about that bite."

"Why? It's like a bee sting. I've had many of them on these hikes with you."

John was laughing now. "Well according to Australian aborigine myths, tribes of people have been turned into bees from the bite of a cuckoo wasp.

"Sure, that plus ten dollars will buy you the Brooklyn Bridge."

Clearly, I was not a position to sell the Brooklyn Bridge, but I had fallen victim to the Australian aboriginal curse. I was now a shiny blue cuckoo wasp.

Well, I might enjoy my transformation, I thought. How about pollinating some flowers? The window was open, and I flew out and away.

From up here, the ground below was so beautiful. This flying is wonderful, I thought. I think I'm going to like my new body, my cuckoo wasp body.

I buzzed around for about thirty minutes before I knew I wanted to do. Yes, that would be fitting, I thought.

Stopping along the way at a few flowers to suck up some nectar for energy, I arrived.

It was closing time and he was walking to his new car. No way I could ever afford a car like that. On his cell phone, probably talking to his wife. Then his assistant approached him. The two were laughing. Then he pulled her close. A passionate kiss followed.

"Oh, Doctor Kelly, what am going to do with you?"

"Well, you can decide when you meet me at my summer cabin this weekend."

My doctor. Doctor Kelly. Jesus, how could he. Bad enough he never called me back, but this with his assistant. That was it.

They were still in a tight embrace when I started my move. Straight down. My wings felt like they were going to break away. The air rushed by me. I was straight on target.

I sank my stinger into his neck. Every drop of venom, give him every drop you have, I thought.

"Jesus, what was that?" he said, grabbing at his neck.

I should let them see me, I thought.

"Dr. Kelly, look at that," she was pointing at me. He looked up and I saw the pain in his eyes.

"Jesus, that damn thing bit me, that God damn bug."

I wanted to speak, but of course I couldn't. I wanted to tell him I was not a bug, I was an insect. But that's okay, because soon he too would suffer the Australian aboriginal curse.

I flew away. My work here is done. Time to look for some flowers to pollinate, after all that's what Cuckoo Wasps do.

Little Pete

The coffee was bitter this morning. Even two extra tablespoons of sugar didn't help.

And the steak was overcooked.

Hell of a way to cook a Texas longhorn, he thought. They'd never do that in Dodge City.

As he lifted his mug, coffee sloshed over the brim and on to his shirt.

His hands were trembling. They had been doing that all morning.

"Calm down. Jesus, I should have stayed in bed," Pete mumbled.

But of course, he couldn't. He had been planning this for weeks, months probably.

He had places to go and people to see.

Yes, 'Little Pete' had places to go and people to see.

But, of course, they weren't expecting him. In fact, if they had known he was coming, they would have been better prepared. Yes, indeed they would have.

He chuckled at the thought.

Nope, he couldn't stay in bed.

His hands continued to tremble.

Little Pete was nothing like his name. At 6 foot 2, 210 pounds, he was definitely not little. Far from it.

The nickname was probably a very logical one since his dad was called 'Big Pete.'

Little Pete took another sip of his coffee. It was not only bitter, but now it was cold too.

He struggled to chew the tough steak.

Not the breakfast he had imagined on this most important day. His most important day.

It was 1890 and he was in what would eventually become the state of Oklahoma.

But that would be about twenty years later.

A year earlier, President Benjamin Harrison had signed a proclamation that two million acres of the region, referred to as Unassigned Lands, would be opened for settlement. Under the provisions of the Homestead Act of 1862, a legal settler could claim 160 acres of public land.

The first Oklahoma Land Rush was to take place on April 22, 1889.

The land was free only to those who could get there first. The hysteria spread. Classified ads appeared in Chicago and New York newspapers calling for meetings of potential settlers.

The border of Oklahoma, where runners were required to wait, was as porous as a border could be. It was more than 300 miles long and, in many places, unmarked. Where it was marked, it was often only with barbed wire or a creek or a pile of stones. And, it was impossible to fully patrol.

Some settlers avoided the patrols and were able to stake their claim before the announced time for the land rush to legally begin. They would eventually be known as the 'Sooners.'

At the break of dawn on April 22,1889, an estimated fifty thousand people waited for the signal to begin the land rush into the Unassigned Lands.

The dramatic moment came when at the stroke of noon starting signals were sounded at the many points of entry.

The afternoon was a day of chaos, excitement, and utter confusion. Men and women rushed to claim homesteads in one of the many new towns that would spring into existence overnight.

But it wasn't just these settlers who jumped at the land rush opportunity, gangs of bandits saw opportunities too.

While the 'wild west' had seen its share of notorious outlaw gangs — from the Dalton Gang to Billy the Kid's Rustlers — smaller gangs, less known, were also at work.

Little Pete wanted to be one of them. An outlaw.

Between the end of the Civil War in 1865 and the Land Rush in 1889, Indian Territory saw thousands of head of cattle cross its prairies and hills. The cattle industry flourished with a surging demand for beef following the war. To move the cattle to market meant getting Texas longhorns to the railheads in Kansas. Those young men driving Texas cattle northward along trail routes were called "cowboys."

One such trail was the Great Western Trail. It ran through the reservations of the Plains Indians in western Indian Territory toward Dodge City. So many cattle were driven along this trail to Dodge City that the city earned the nickname "cow capital of the world."

Unfortunately, Dodge City, as a cow-town, was a wild place especially when the cowboys arrived with their herds. Saloons, gambling establishments, dancing halls and brothels were particularly active. Too active for the normal town folk.

Thus, law enforcement personnel became part of Dodge City, and Big Pete joined forces with the likes of lawmen such as Bat Masterson and Wyatt Earp to deal with the unruly cowboys.

Big Pete eventually became known as 'Marshal Big Pete,' to the Dodge City community.

By the mid 1880s, the cattle drives were dwindling for many reasons. More land was being fenced, herds were being raised in Indian Territory, and Kansas enacted quarantine laws that restricted access. The final stake in the heart of cattle drives was the railroads themselves. As the rail lines moved south into Texas, the need to drive cattle north ended.

Dodge City, no longer a cow town, settled into a more peaceful wheat farming community.

Little Pete, however, yearned for something more exciting than watching Red Winter Wheat grow. All he had to do was look to the south. To the Oklahoma territory.

When the Oklahoma Territory was opened in 1889, banks were some of the first businesses established. Within a few days of the land rush, at least nine were opened. One of these, the Oklahoma Bank, was started in a tent. Renamed First National Bank of Oklahoma City in 1890, the bank moved into a wooden building at the corner of Main and Broadway streets.

Little Pete was well aware of the opportunities presented by banks in the Oklahoma City area.

Taking another sip of the bitter coffee, he heard her.

"Something wrong with your steak, honey?"

It was the young waitress. She had been watching him all morning, ever since he sat down at the small table by the window.

"Oh no, it's fine. Just not hungry I reckon."

"Well let me know if you need anything, anything at all, honey," she replied.

As she turned to leave, she winked, but he was so busy thinking about the day ahead that he failed to notice.

I could sure use a load of nerves, Little Pete thought, as he looked down at his trembling hands. Yeah, a covered wagon full of nerves is what I need.

He slowly glanced up and looked across Main Street. The wind was picking up and dust was blowing everywhere. Still, he could see it, directly across from him.

The First National Bank of Oklahoma.

The tent was long gone. There was a new building in its place.

A tent would have been easier, he thought. Much easier.

The bank was closed now but would open in thirty minutes. He would be there when it did. And when he entered, he would finally become an outlaw. Finally.

He had planned the day down to the last detail, but still he felt uneasy.

Probably because it's my first ... bank heist, he thought.

As the clock above the bar approached nine, he took a deep breath. Almost time as he placed a shiny new silver dollar on the table. The portrait of Lady Liberty seemed to be looking right at him, almost like she knew what he was about to do. Perhaps she wanted to tell him to leave right now and head back to the safety of the wheat farm in Dodge City.

"Too late for that," he mumbled as he headed for the exit.

It was a wide street. Main Street. Nothing but dirt and horse crap.

Welcome to Oklahoma City, he thought, as he carefully navigated across the street to the First National Bank of Oklahoma.

Oklahoma City, a place founded on a single afternoon, with the Land Rush, when a formerly empty patch of prairie became a city of 10,000. The empty patch was a perfect place for a town. It was right where railroad tracks crossed a river, and so it drew settlers like a magnet.

Within days there were wooden houses, slapped together out of preassembled frames. And banks. Nine banks had opened since the Land Rush.

And now Little Pete was aiming to empty one of its banks.

As Little Pete approached the doors of the First National Bank of Oklahoma, he tapped the Colt 45 revolver holstered on his right hip.

Funny, he thought, the same cream handled gun that Wyatt Earp carried. His dad, Big Pete, too. And now he carried one, into the lobby of the First National Bank of Oklahoma.

The lobby was full of early morning customers. Many were standing in line waiting for their turn with the bank teller. Some were just visiting and chatting with one another. He didn't see a guard.

Forgetting to pull out his Colt 45, Little Pete started shouting. As he did people turned in his direction.

He had practiced many times what he wanted to say. Now it was time. Just say it, he said to himself.

"Good morning, everyone. Can I have your attention. No need to panic. Stay calm ... I'm here to ...."

But he couldn't finish his sentence. He choked, then he started over,

"Damn it, everyone, listen up," he was shouting at the top of his voice and his hands were shaking.

An old man to his left, stepped forward and spoke,

"What is it, young man, what do you want to say?"

"Yes, yes, what is it," others chimed in.

"Jesus Christ ... I'm here to ... can't you see ... I'm here to ..."

Before he could finish, he heard a voice directly behind him,

"What are you here for Little Pete?"

"Huh?"

"Please tell us what you intend to do."

Little Pete turned around in the direction of the voice. He knew that voice, but how. How was he here?

"Perhaps you're here to open an account? Yes, I bet that's why you're here."

It was his dad, Big Pete. Standing there. But how?

Little Pete was speechless. He took a few steps back.

His dad continued,

"I guess you want to deposit your profits from this year's wheat harvest in this brand new bank. Yes, that must be it. That must be it ... son."

"But" was all Little Pete could finally say.

"But I think you left your money back at the boarding house across the street, so let me give you something to open your new account.

"But how ..."

"Lucky, I happened to be here in Oklahoma City, wouldn't you agree?"

"But dad, you ... you ... died ... in a gunfight ... with the Dalton gang four years ago..."

Big Pete smiled. Then he approached Little Pete.

"Doesn't mean I haven't been watching out for you."

"Huh?"

"I'll always be watching out for you, son. That's what dad's do."

Little Pete just stood there, looking at his dad. As he did memories of years gone by ran through his mind.

Memories like his dad teaching him how to ride a horse, how to fire a gun, how to drink whiskey, how to treat a woman, how to ...

Suddenly his dad spoke,

"Here, catch, deposit this."

Little Pete saw it flipping towards him. It was shiny and silver. It was a new silver dollar.

As he reached out to catch it, he could have sworn that Lady Liberty was smiling at him.

The coin bounced off his outstretched hand and fell to the floor.

Little Pete reached down to pick it up.

He had so much to ask his dad, so many questions.

But when he looked up, Big Pete was gone.

The Other Ones

I opened my eyes, but I couldn't see. It was still dark inside. Dark in our space.

I felt the urge, so I crawled out of the of dark space onto the ledge outside.

As I stood there, the little wet ones from the land above hit my uncovered body. They were not warm this time. I felt little bumps rising on my arms.

Thank goodness for the wet ones. They gave us drink and made the things that we ate grow and turn green.

But sometimes, the wet ones went away for a long time. When they did the green things turned brown and we couldn't eat. Those were terrible times when many would fall asleep and never wake up.

I didn't know from where the falling wet ones came but thought it might be from the unknown land high above us. I didn't know why sometimes the wet ones were soft and just floated from the land above, covering the place we stood on. It was very cold when I felt it and when I stood in it. But after a while it would be gone.

In the distance, I could see the bright flickering. Many flickerings. Those other ones were the fortunate ones, I thought, they can see when the dark comes and feel warm in the cold that we, on this side of the deep valley, can't.

We wanted the source of light and heat, but they would not give it to us.

They even had more green things to eat. But they wouldn't share.

The other ones didn't care that we shivered and went hungry. We didn't know why. Were we that different?

I looked up to the dark land above and to the many small and bright sparkles that lived there. Very small, like small points. They had moved slightly since last night, especially the big round one which was brighter than all the small ones.

All moved, except for one in the dark land above. It never did. It was always in the same place in the dark land above. It always pointed in the same direction and helped us return home when it was dark.

Suddenly, I heard the loud noise of the four legged one. The fast one, the scary one, the one with the large sharp points in its mouth. The one that was covered in the long things that grew on top of me. The four legged one that took our little one away.

Our little one never returned. The four legged one had taken many from our side of the valley, especially our little ones and the old ones. They never came back.

But after a while another little one arrived.

I started shaking as the noise from the four legged one came closer. I was afraid. Would I be taken away like our little one?

Suddenly the big bright warm circle appeared from behind the tall land on the other side of the valley. All the small sparkles above me were gone. And the big round one too, was gone. But we knew they would be back when the bright circle disappeared to the tall hills on our side of the valley.

With the arrival of the bright circle, the land above changed. There was light and I could see deep into the valley below. I could also feel a growing warmth on my uncovered body. The wet ones covering my body slowly vanished. I felt good.

This big bright warm circle was important too. The growing things needed it to grow and turn green. I think we needed it too, but I wasn't sure why.

The big circle was there to chase away the dark, except for the one time when, high above us, it slowly disappeared. All that remained was a faint outline of the circle. We were all scared then when the sparkles appeared in the land above. Even those on the other side of the valley were afraid. Those with the flickerings and much green to eat were afraid.

But, after a while the big circle returned. It grew from a small dot to a big circle. We didn't know where it had gone, but we were so happy that it decided to come back to us. We all fell to our knees and gave thanks for its return. We gave it a name to show our happiness. We called it "sunn." The big bright circle was now the sunn.

Back into the space I crawled. The light from the sunn entered with me.

The other one was still on the ground. The other one was different from me. Very different. I felt good when the other one was close and sometimes, I had strange feelings for the other one.

It was from inside the other one that our little one came. The little ones that made strange sounds. That ate from the bumps of the other one. I didn't understand, but many of us had little ones. After a while, the little ones would look like us.

The other one rose and pointed to the entrance to the ledge. "Ooout." it said.

I shook my head.

"Nooo ooout."

The other one started for the ledge. I stood in the way.

The other one stopped.

"Ooout."

I made a sound like the four-legged one. "Raaaaaw." I pointed to the outside.

The other one turned and went to the darkness in the back of the space.

The little one was up now. She was pointing at her mouth.

"Fuood."

I handed her some of the green stuff.

The little one had that strange look on her face, its mouth turned up at the corners. Then it made another strange sound. "Ha, ha, ha." When it did that, we knew the little one was happy. We were too.

Since the wet ones falling from above had stopped, we all crawled out onto the ledge. Then we saw it. It was a mystery, but there it was, again. A half circle, so far away, with different colors, but always the same colors. Unlike the sunn, it didn't hurt to look at it. It was beautiful. Soon it disappeared.

There was much wet in the valley below and it was moving fast along the valley floor. Once I went down there to touch the moving wet and it grabbed me and pushed me far down the valley to a land I had never seen before. I didn't get back to my other one until the sunn appeared three times in the unknown land above.

Suddenly the sunn disappeared behind large dark islands floating in the land above. Then from the land above a flash of bright light with a long tail falling into the valley followed by a loud noise, like giant hands coming together. The wet ones appeared again. It was time to seek the safety of the dark space.

It was a time when we huddled together, the other one, the little one, and me. When the flashes with a long tail and the noises came. We were afraid. The little one made loud noises and much wet fell from its eyes. The little one was not happy.

We were afraid that the mysterious land above, which we could never travel to, was mad at us, but we didn't know why. We didn't know what to do make it happy again. How to make it stop.

But then the sunn appeared, and the loud noise was gone. The large falling wet ones too, had stopped.

The light from sunn reached inside our space.

The little one was standing, facing the hard wall. The scratching on the wall revealed one that looked like me. Next to it was the four legged one. It was so real what the little one had scratched into the hard wall. But I wondered would anyone ever see it, enjoy it, what the little one had scratched on the wall.

I wondered about a lot of things lately.

I wondered why we were here on this land below the unknown land above. On this land that we called "erth." Where had we been before? Where would we be after the sunn had appeared more times than I could imagine? I had no answers, just questions.

Perhaps, that's why I was here? To think, to question, to wonder. Perhaps it was as simple as that.

I felt the urge again and went out on the ledge. The warmth of the sunn covered my naked body. I felt good, and then the sound came from deep within me.

"Ha, ha, ha."

I knew I was happy.

The Dummy

I looked up. I was sitting on his lap. Tom's lap. Like so many nights before.

"And how are you feeling tonight, Charlie?" Tom's lips were moving.

"I'm not feeling anything. Numb from head to toe."

"Fell off the wagon, again?"

"It was more like a beer truck."

The laughter exploded throughout the darkened room. The only light was from above.

I waved my small arms above my head. Tom rolled his eyes.

"Charlie, I thought your wife told you to stop drinking?"

"Well, we agreed that I would only drink on days starting with the letter T."

"Well, that sounds reasonable, Charlie."

"I thought so too, but she still got angry with me. Real angry."

"Why?"

"She didn't care for me drinking on Tuesday, Thursday, Today and Tomorrow."

More laughter. Clapping too. I was on a roll. It felt good.

"Hey Tom, knock, knock."

"Okay, who's there Charlie?"

"Wooden shoe."

"Wooden shoe who?"

"Wooden shoe like to hear another joke?"

Some laughter and many groans filled the room.

"Do I have a choice?"

"Tom, did I tell you that my dog ate my scrabble letters?"

"Oh, I'm so sorry, Charlie. Is he okay?"

"Not sure, but he keeps leaving me messages around the house."

After twenty minutes, our show was over.

The stage lights brightened.

The audience broke out in applause as we exited right.

The applause continued, so we decided it was time for an encore.

Returning to the stage, I once again settled onto Tom's lap.

"Well, that was a quick break," Tom said looking down at me.

"Speaking of breaks ..."

"What about them, Charlie?"

"I heard that some people broke into your house a couple of nights ago?"

"I'd rather not talk about it."

"And I also heard they couldn't find anything of value, so they left some stuff for you."

We had been doing this act for ten years now. New jokes, old jokes, just Tom and me. Las Vegas mostly, sometimes Reno.

"Hey Tom, your doctor confided in me that the problem isn't that obesity runs in your family."

"Oh, so what is it? What did he say?" said Tom patting his rather large belly.

"He said that the problem is that no one runs in your family."

The audience responded with subdued laughter. Strange, I thought, that was one of my favorite jokes. Perhaps it's just tonight's crowd. Tough crowd.

"Hey Charlie, I heard that you've found a new girlfriend."

"Yes, I have."

"So, how's the relationship?"

"Like a teepee."

"What?"

"It's in tents."

"I'm so happy for you, Charlie."

"Thanks Tom, but I'm not sure it's going to last."

"Why, Charlie, why do you think that?"

"Well to begin with, she's a lawyer."

"So?"

"And she's starting to lose her appeal."

Scattered groans filled the room. Little laughter.

"Tough crowd tonight, Charlie."

"Speaking of tough, Tom."

"Yes?"

"In these tough times, it's nice to see that Taco Bell is providing more value than ever."

"How's that, Charlie?"

"Where else can you get gas for $1.19?"

More groans.

"Hey Charlie, how's your family been?"

"I'm glad you asked Tom. My grandfather has been through an unbelievably tough time. As a young boy, he worked in a salt mine. Later when he was in the big war, he survived a mustard gas attack. And recently during a protest march he was hit with pepper spray by the police."

"Oh my gosh, Charlie, is he okay?"

"Better than okay cause now he's more than a war veteran."

"Oh?"

"Yeah, now he's a seasoned veteran."

More loud groans from the audience. Perhaps we're getting too old, too stale, for this I thought.

"Hey Tom, I understand you're getting married."

"Yes, Charlie, at long last."

"Well, have you introduced your bride to be to your mom yet?"

"Oh, yes indeed."

"Well, how did that go?"

"Well, we were invited to dinner."

"How nice."

"So, I showed up with three girls."

"Three?"

"Yes, three, and I lined them up facing my mother."

"Go on."

"And I asked my mom to guess which one I was marrying."

"And?"

"And she pointed to the one on the left and said that one."

"And?"

"And I said mom you're correct, how did you know?"

"What did she say?"

"She said she could tell because she disliked her when she first saw her."

Much laughter broke out. Time to exit, I thought. On a high note.

"Thank you, Tom and, of course, Charlie for a wonderful performance this evening." It was the MC. He walked out on to the stage, applauding. The audience took up his cue and started applauding too. Probably because they wanted us to leave.

Tom lifted me up and we walked off the stage.

The door to our dressing room closed. Another night was coming to an end. Time to pack up.

Suddenly there was a knock at the door.

"I have your dinner, can I come in?"

"Sure."

The door opened and a young man carrying a tray entered.

"Shall I put it on the table?"

"Sure. Thanks."

"By the way, great performance tonight."

"Thanks, but sometimes I wonder if we are getting out of touch with our audiences."

"Perhaps you just need new material or ..."

"A new dummy?"

"Well, yeah that too."

"Thinking about it."

"By the way, Charlie, where's Tom?"

"Oh, I've already stuffed him in his storage box. I'll take Tom out tomorrow before our performance."

Loki's Secret Decoder Club

"Eldon, you best start eating, or you'll be late for school."

It was my mom. I heard her voice, but I wasn't paying any attention.

"Eldon, did you hear me?"

"Err, sorry mom."

"What did I say?"

"Sorry mom, I was ..."

"Daydreaming!"

"No."

"Well, whatever, but you better finish that cereal cause the school bus will coming by any minute."

"Yes, mom."

My focus had been elsewhere all morning at the breakfast table. It was a cereal that I pulled from the store shelves. There was only one box, sitting in the back behind the Corn Flakes.

Loki's Mystery Crunch.

I was attracted to the bright orange packaging and the drawings of flying creatures.

On the side of the extra-large box, in bold print the company claimed that no two bowls of Loki's taste the same. This was true. My first bowl was banana almond flavor, the next like rusty nails, other times it tasted like someone's damp seashell collection.

Whatever the taste, I was hooked. I couldn't get enough.

But this morning it wasn't the flying creatures, or this morning's molasses taste of the soggy popcorn-like texture. It was the offer on the back of the box.

Loki's Secret Decoder Club.

Only $5.

The offer continued.

Only available for those 10 and under. A secret message will be sent to you each week, with instructions on how to decode it. Loads of fun for the very young.

Now I was hooked on the Secret Decoder Club.

Gulping down the last of the bowl of cereal, which had mysteriously changed to a moldy drywall flavor, I turned to my mom.

"Mom."

"What now Eldon?"

"For my birthday, I know what I'd like."

"Later, Eldon, you need to get to school."

All day at school, all I could think of was the Secret Decoder Club.

Even when I was on the bus headed back home, the Secret Decoder Club kept rolling around in my head.

"Hey, Eldon, you getting off at your stop, or riding to the end of the line?"

It was the school bus driver, Mr. Reed. The tone of his voice was one of frustration with a touch of anger.

The bus had stopped in front of our house, but I was in another world. The world of Loki. Of course, I couldn't tell Mr. Reed. Nope, only those 10 and under.

As I struggled to retrieve my backpack which had fallen under the seat in front of me, Mr. Reed let out a loud grunt. We all knew it was his way of swearing and doing it in a way which would not get him suspended.

Dashing to the front of the bus, I wanted to stop and thank Mr. Reed, but as I got closer, he let out another grunt, so I simply exited.

The house was empty, but there was a note on the kitchen table. Mom had to go into town for a prescription and she'd be back soon. Her note was right next to the box of Loki's Mystery Crunch.

Tossing mom's note aside, I turned my attention to the box of cereal.

The flying creatures on the front looked like men, strange men, with wings and long horns. Some had spears, others sharp pointed fingers. Some were laughing, others had an ominous look. But they all looked like they were flying to the bold red letters,

CEREAL OF THE ANCIENT NORWEGIANS.

"Wow," I muttered. I hadn't seen that before. Cereal of the ancient Norwegians. Who knew?

Perhaps my dad would know.

Dad once told me that during the 19th century, political and economic pressures drove thousands of Norwegians to move to the United States and like his grandfather, many settled in Iowa.

Many of these immigrants from Norway had been farmers, so it was only natural that they continued farming in Iowa. In fact, this farm we lived on, that my dad worked, was settled by his grandfather's family in the decade after the Civil War.

"Immigrants from Norway, in search of a better life during the recession," my dad reminded me.

"They left their small farm in central Norway and made the one-week journey to America on a cramped steamship, called the Hellig Olav."

Turning the cereal box over, the following instructions jumped out at me:

Limited time, act now.

Send $5 and Loki will rush his mystery messages to you.

And then in bold print,

BUT TELL NO ONE.

Just then my mom opened the front door.

"Oh, Eldon, I thought I could get home before you. Sorry."

"That's okay, mom."

"How was school."

"Fine."

"What are you doing this afternoon?"

"Nothing."

"You could help your dad. I saw him on the tractor when I drove in."

"I think I'll do some homework."

"Sure, you best do that."

As I headed up the stairs to my bedroom, I wondered why I said that to mom. I didn't have any homework.

But of course, I certainly couldn't tell her that the last thing I wanted to do was spend the rest of the day in our corn fields.

But that's the way it is, I thought, living on a farm in north central Iowa. 10 miles from town and 3 miles to the closest neighbor. Miles of corn, every way you looked. Corn, corn, corn.

And that's all my dad could talk about.

"You should be proud to be one of the 200,000 Iowa farms producing corn. And did I ever tell you Eldon, Iowa is number one in corn production. Number one, Eldon."

Of course, he had told me, number one, more times than I could remember, especially around mid-September harvest time and April planting.

"It's the soil, Eldon, we are blessed with some of the richest farmland on the planet."

It never seemed to end. Corn conversations.

"Make sure you put some extra butter on that sweet corn, Eldon. It really brings out the flavor."

Funny thing too, I didn't even like the stuff. But of course, I didn't dare tell dad.

"Hey Eldon, you know many kernels are on that ear you're about to eat? Around 800, Eldon. can you believe that?"

And so, it went on. And on. No wonder I wanted to join Loki's Secret Decoder Club. I was bored here. Corn bored.

Even when I asked dad if we could get one of those new television sets that some of my friends in school were talking about, he replied that it was the work of the devil and his dad's upright RCA radio was good enough for us.

When I tried to convince him that Saturday morning television shows like The Adventures of Superman and Howdy Doody were not the work of the devil, he simply closed the conversation with the following reply,

"And why would we want to watch television when we can all listen to Jack Benny, Red Skelton, or Father Knows Best? Why?"

Of course, dad really didn't expect me to answer why, so I just resigned myself that I would have to grow up without Captain Kangaroo, or the Mouseketeers.

When having dinner that night — corn soup, of course — mom brought up my morning statement about my upcoming birthday.

"So, Eldon, you've decided what you'd like for your birthday?"

Remembering the bold print on the box, I replied, "I thought I did, but I've changed my mind. Still thinking."

That night, in the safety of my bedroom, I stuffed a brand new five-dollar bill, the one that I got for my last birthday, in an envelope along with a note to Loki with our address.

As my tongue teased the dry envelope glue to life a chill ran through my body. I was really doing it. Joining Loki's Secret Decoder Club. My boring life would be over, thanks to Loki.

Sneaking down to the living room, I opened the desk drawer and found a single stamp. It was a 3-cent stamp. A picture of a half-shucked ear of corn and the words Sweet Corn, USA.

How appropriate, I thought, not realizing at the time that my dad was saving that stamp. A special corn stamp.

The school bus dropped us off in front of school and just down the street was a mailbox. I sprinted there, depositing my envelope to the Loki Mystery Crunch Company, and back.

"What was that all about?" It was my best friend, Michael.

Michael was 11, so I had to be careful with my reply.

"Nothing. Just a little exercise this morning."

After school, for the next two weeks, when the school bus dropped me off, I first ran to the mailbox looking for my package.

And then one Friday afternoon, it was there. An envelope addressed to Eldon Johansen.

Securing the envelope between the pages of my math textbook, I carried the rest of the mail to the kitchen table. Mom was there.

"Eldon, what's gotten into you, bringing in the mail every afternoon?"

"Just trying to help out, Mom."

"Well, would you like some cookies and milk before dinner. Chocolate chip, your favorite."

"No thanks, mom, I'm going up to my room to do some math homework."

As I turned, I noticed the look of surprise on mom's face. It was, after all, the first time I had turned down her chocolate chip cookies.

But I couldn't wait.

Up the stairs, two steps at a time, and I was finally alone, in the privacy of my bedroom. Well, perhaps not alone, as I clutched at the envelope from Loki.

Strange, I thought, there was no return address. Just the name Loki in the upper left corner. And the stamp was missing.

I gently opened the envelope, taking care not to tear any of the precious contents.

Two smaller envelopes fell out and on to the floor. One was marked secret message and the other message decoder.

Opening the secret message envelope, I discovered a piece of paper with a series of numbers.

2/27 # 5/22/13/26/31 # ...

Occasionally there appeared a

#

The second enveloped produced a list of numbers each corresponding to a particular letter. It looked like this,

2 h

5 e

13 d

22 l

27 i

31 n

36 o

It also noted that the symbol # was a period and the start of a new sentence.

The instructions simply said to pair up the numbers on the secret message with the decoder letter list.

And so, as I solved the secret message my adventure with Loki began.

The decoded message was short, but it tugged at me. Struggling to contain my excitement, I read the full message to myself.

"hi eldon. welcome to my secret decoder club. every week you will receive a letter from me. we should have a great time together. your friend loki."

And so, every Friday, I would jump off the school bus and run full speed to the mailbox. And every Friday, Loki's letter was there. Every Friday. A letter without a stamp and without a return address.

And every Friday I would excuse myself, head up to my room, secure the door, and start decoding.

For the first month, the decoded messages from Loki were wonderful. At long last, I had a friend. At last, I was not bored. I even found myself liking corn.

But then, I received a very strange message. It actually frightened me as I decoded and read it.

"dear eldon. our time for secret messages is over. this will be my last message. im sad to write you that tomorrow at noon, our planet as we know it will cease to exist. i advise you to take care. a new world will appear where dogs will rule the earth. good bye. loki."

The decoded message fell from my hands. I was confused. What should I do? What could I do?

At dinner I was especially quiet.

"Eldon, has the cat got your tongue? Nothing to say. That's not like you."

"What?" I was thinking of the secret message and barely heard mom.

"Are you feeling okay, son?" It was dad.

"Just tired, dad. Just tired."

"Well, finish your corn chowder, and head up to bed."

Suddenly the corn didn't appeal to me, just like before Loki's letters. But I forced it down and excused myself.

"And don't forget to brush your teeth, young man."

Why bother, I thought, as I pushed my chair back against the table.

Tossing and turning all night, into the early morning as the approaching sun slowly lit up my bedroom. Usually, I enjoyed the early morning sun, the start of a new day. But not today. No, definitely not today.

Time was moving fast. Too fast. Noon was near.

Suddenly, dark, ominous storm clouds appeared to the west. They quickly engulfed the bright sky above. The sun disappeared. The winds picked up. Mom turned on the kitchen lights. It was almost noon.

Dad came running in from the fields. He was covered in corn dust. He had a panicked look.

Struggling to get his words out, he finally said.

"Quick everyone. To the tornado shelter. There's a big one coming."

The tornado shelter was a simple underground dirt enclosure, only a few yards from the house. We had used it on a few occasions. But this was the first-time dad seemed so concerned, so frightened actually.

As he struggled to lift open the heavy wooden doors, I looked behind me.

There it was, barreling down on us.

Three of them. Gigantic columns of violently twisting air rotating around each other. Picking up everything it their path.

And we were in their path.

The wind started spinning around us.

The trees creaked loudly as if they were announcing their impending doom. Even the strongest trees were helpless against the intense wind. Swirling dust filled the air and pounded against my bare skin. My face felt like it was on fire.

The sound was like an oncoming freight train, but louder. So much louder. My ears popped.

The ground started shaking. I felt I was walking on a giant sponge. I fought to stay upright.

Finally, I dropped down into the shelter.

Dad let the heavy doors fall shut. For a moment it was quiet, but then the sounds returned. Splitting trees. Pounding on the shelter's wooden doors above, like the tornado wanted in, wanted us.

I started crying.

"Don't worry, Eldon, it'll be okay. You're safe down here." It was dad.

Wiping the falling tears from my cheeks, I knew I had to confess.

"It was me dad, I'm sorry."

"What are you talking about?"

"It was me; I took the stamp you were saving."

"Oh, don't worry, Eldon, I can always get more."

"I just needed one stamp. And that was the only one I could find."

"Really, Eldon. Why did you need a stamp?"

As the shelter's wooden doors began to rattle against the fierce wind, I realized it was time to tell them about Loki and the secret messages.

And I did. Everything, even the last letter, which I had in my pocket.

I pulled it out, uncrumpled it, and handed to dad.

As he read it, dust started falling through the doors above. The tornadoes sounded like they were right above us. Stomping on the ground above us. Wanting in.

"Eldon, who sent you this?"

"Loki. I found him on the back of Loki's mystery crunch cereal. The cereal of the ancient Norwegians."

"Loki? Ancient Norway?" My dad replied.

"Yes, why?"

"Det er en spøk." He was laughing now. My dad was laughing.

Although mom knew a few Norwegian phrases, I could tell dad's reply had her confused.

"What is it, Eric?" It was my mom.

"It's a joke, the secret messages are a joke."

"How do you know?"

"In Norse mythology, Loki is best known as the trickster god. Loki is a chaos god. In Norway, you wouldn't pray to Loki; you would pray to the other gods to keep Loki away."

"Oh."

"Someone's played a joke on you, Eldon."

"But the tornadoes at noon, and …"

"Sure, and dogs taking over the world. It's a joke Eldon, one big joke. That's all."

Finally, the storm had passed, and it was time to open the wooden doors.

"Come on, Eldon. We probably have some cleaning up to do."

Pushing up the heavy wooden doors, dad was laughing. A big smile on his face.

"End of the world. Nothing but dogs," he said looking at me.

The doors slowly swung open. The sun was shining. The violent wind had turned into a gentle breeze.

Suddenly dad's smile turned to confusion. His eyes tightened. His mouth opened wide.

We both heard the approaching noise.

Dogs, it sounded like hundreds, perhaps thousands, of them. Barking, growling as they approached our open tornado shelter.

The Edge

The hike was proving more difficult than I had expected. And it was getting dark and there would be no moon tonight.

It was my first hike of the season. My first hike since I put my gear away last fall.

Reaching for my water bottle, I could tell I was running low. I knew I should have filled up at that stream at lunchtime. But, as usual, I didn't.

Always pushing myself to the edge. How close can I get before I fall off? Not literally of course. With the water, I told myself I'm sure to find another stream. But for the rest of the afternoon, there were no streams to be found. So now, as darkness approached, I was getting close to the edge.

And why did I neglect to take the trail map the park ranger had offered. "You might need this. Hikers get lost up there."

"No thanks, I already have one." But I didn't. And I knew I didn't. That damn edge again.

"You're going to get hurt, or worse," my friends would tell me. I wouldn't listen.

Even when I was just a kid, I pushed myself. How far can I take this? My parents just dismissed it at first.

"He's just a kid, let him try it," they would say to their friends. "After all, he's got to learn and what better way to learn than trying."

And so, I pushed and pushed, closer and closer to that edge.

Jumping off the backyard tree. How high could I go before jumping off? Should I try the next branch up? How close can I get to the top? All the way?

"It's a bad sprain," the doctor said, "just keep him out of trees." They all laughed, but I didn't. I knew it was the edge, and it would always be. It had to be. Always reaching for the next branch.

But then one day, I got too close.

It was the sharpest knife I could find. My mom's prized kitchen knife, too. A Miyabi knife, which she purchased on our holiday in Japan.

Holding the smooth wood handle, I noticed how solid, how comfortable it felt in my hand. The glistening floral pattern on the blade caught my attention too. How beautiful, I thought.

I remember my dad saying, "but it's $400 dollars."

She convinced him, and they brought it home. Now I was holding it and wondering.

What if I stand straight up, hold the knife out, drop it towards my bare foot? How close can I get to my toes? What if I closed one eye? Two eyes? What if I spun around first? What if?

"How in the hell did he do it?" the doctor was looking at the knife protruding from the top of my right foot. "Jesus he just missed the tibial artery. What a mess that would have been."

As the doctor removed my mother's $400 Miyabi knife from my foot, I thought to myself, how the hell did I do it was not the right question. The right question was why, and the answer, as always, was the edge.

The sun had set. It was almost dark now and the temperature was falling.

I reached in my backpack and felt it. A flashlight. Then a candy bar. One small candy bar. At least it was something to eat.

"Going to the edge never meant not eating," I said, not expecting anyone to hear.

As the dark milk chocolate caressed my lips, I heard the sound. Like a snapping branch.

"Anyone there?" I said peering into the darkness.

I reached for the flashlight and clicked the switch.

"Shit, the batteries must be dead."

I shook the flashlight; it was so light. Too light. "My God, the batteries are missing."

Then I realized, I forgot to put in new batteries this morning to replace the old ones I had removed at the end the hiking season last year.

Did I really forget? Was it the damn edge again?

Snap. That sound again. Behind me. Close too.

Matches, did I pack any?

Fumbling in the dark, thrashing around in my backpack, there it was. Probably left over from years ago when I use to set up campfires.

A box of matches. Opening the cover, reaching in, I realized there was only three or four wooden matches in the box. Forgot to replace those too, I thought.

I removed one match and struck it on the side of the box. Sparks, then a small flame.

Holding the burning wooden match in my hand, I stood up.

The light flickered against the tall trees in front of me. I slowly turned. More trees, deep dense underbrush.

Holding the match out as far as I could, I thought I saw movement.

"Anyone there?" I shouted again. And again, no response.

"Damn!" My voice rose to the sound of a hundred exclamation points. The burning match had reached my fingers. "Damn, edge, God damn edge."

I sat down. Hungry. Perhaps there's more food in my pack? But I didn't want to light one of my remaining matches to look.

But there was more. I could feel it.

A stick of gum. One damn stick of gum.

The wrapper was stuck to the gum. As I peeled it away, I wondered, how old is this gum? I haven't chewed gum for years. My dentist told me to give it up. Yes, when did he tell me that? Five, ten years ago.

The gum was hard and stale. Whatever flavor it had was long gone.

"This is useless," I screamed, spitting the gum into the dark night.

What time is it? I wondered, as I checked the display on my old Fitbit. It was only ten, but at least I had done 25,000 steps. I chuckled.

Then the snap again, more than one this time. Like something or someone was moving in the brush behind me.

Another match came to life. Something moved? Or was it simply shadows dancing in the slight breeze. "God damn edge," I screamed into the returning darkness as the match flickered its last. "God damn edge."

Hours passed. It was now after midnight. And it was colder. I was colder.

A simple sweatshirt, that's all I would need, I thought. But no, you wanted to rough it. Just a light shirt will be fine. And shorts. Jesus, my legs were cold. And I was thirsty. I had consumed the last of my water hours ago. "You idiot, damn you, you idiot." I screamed.

Snap. But not just a snap this time. A grunt too. Yes, there was something out there in the darkness.

I was panicking now. Like the panic attacks I would get before any big exam in college. Pills didn't help. Nor did meditation. Mindfulness was useless. I thought they were over after college. But here I was, lost in a dark forest in the middle of a full-blown panic attack.

My arms went numb. My breathing became shallow and rapid. Sweating now. My heart was racing, pounding in my chest. Dizzy and confused. I was losing control. Just like college. I felt I was going to die, but of course, as my therapist had said, "that's not going to happen. At the extreme, you'll faint, but you won't die."

"Flight, or fight," she said. "That's what it's all about. Your panic attacks. A stress reaction traced back to the survival needs of your early ancestors."

Slowly making my way in a direction away from the noise, with my hands outstretched in front of me, I shouted, "Damn ancestors."

But it wasn't them, those cave dwellers who were terrorized by the unknown during those moonless nights.

It was me. Now it was me.

I'm not sure how long I stumbled through that dark forest. How many trees I ran into? How many times I hit my head on low hanging branches, how many times I twisted my ankles on concealed rocks, how many cuts and bruises on my exposed legs and arms?

"Why the hell did I pick a moonless night?" I struck my last match against the box. The wooden match broke in two and fell to the ground.

"Jesus, what else could possibly go wrong?"

Exhausted, I decided to sit down. The ground was soft. Inviting, I thought.

"I'll just stay here until the sun comes up. Not one step further. I'm done with flight."

As I slumped back, my head touched the grass. So smooth, like a pillow.

My eyes were getting heavy now, I was slipping into a dreamy sleep state. My body wasn't resisting. Let go, I thought.

Just before my eyes closed, I whispered to the darkness in front of me. "The edge, it'll be the end of me. Damn edge." Then I was sound asleep.

The sound of birds above me. "Probably vultures," I chuckled, "out for breakfast?"

I could feel the warm sun against my face. I was okay now. The panic attack was long gone.

I rubbed my eyes, letting in the morning sun.

Strange, my legs were hanging down, being pulled down. Why was that?

Sitting up, looking straight ahead, I recoiled back. "What the hell?"

I had fallen asleep at the edge of a cliff. My legs were dangling over the edge. Here at the edge of the Grand Canyon. The north side, with its dense forest.

Looking down I could see the Colorado River, hundreds of feet below. The Colorado River, with its raging rapids, straight down from where I was sitting. Straight down from where I had decided to stop in the darkness last night. Where I decided I would not take one more step.

"Makes perfect sense," I said, "I just had to end up at the edge."

The Test

The doorbell rang. She was at the front door. Crying.

"Can I come in?" She pleaded. "Please. No one has to know."

"I'm sorry, but you know the regulations," I replied.

She was my younger sister, Cathy. I had not seen her since she was a little girl, and she was sent away.

"But I have no place to hide and it's cold out here," she said.

And it was. Cold. It was snowing too. The wispy fog she exhaled, and her constant shivering revealed the bitter cold outside. Still, I hesitated to unlock the door. The authorities, I thought.

"Please, I'm freezing. I'll die out here."

It was evening and I couldn't tell if anyone was watching, but I decided I couldn't let her freeze out there. She was my sister after all. I looked beyond her, into the darkness and opened the door.

"Quick, get in here before anyone sees you. I don't want to get reported. The damn neighbors are always on the lookout for ..." I decided best not to continue.

She rushed inside and fell on the floor. I turned out the light.

"Hopefully no one saw you."

She didn't answer. I reached down and helped her to her feet.

"Let's go into the kitchen. I'll get you something hot to drink. But first, let me close the curtains."

With the kitchen curtains closed, I sat her at the table and then went to the stove. She was shivering.

"Coffee, tea, hot chocolate?"

"Hot chocolate, thank you."

Of course, hot chocolate. Hot chocolate was Cathy's favorite drink, even in summertime. I remember she was drinking hot chocolate the day the authorities arrived to "remove her from the premises." It was early morning.

When she was born, the doctors, as required, reported her birth, and thus the authorities were alerted. My parents were told she was put on the "watch list," to be tested.

The hot chocolate was ready. I carried the warm mug to the table.

"Five years," the authorities said," she will have to be tested at the age of five, like everyone." The authorities would return then.

Of course, I had been tested too. And I passed. So, I didn't go to the facilities. My parents were so relieved. But then, years later when my sister was tested, she failed. Cathy failed. They were shocked.

"Look at these results, she definitely failed," the authorities told my parents. "No way she can function in society. We will have to institutionalize her and attempt to reprogram her. Hopefully, she will be able to return to society.

"Please, please, let her stay," my parents cried out.

"But it's for her own good. Yours too," they replied. "She will not be happy on the outside, until she is able to adjust."

And so, they took her away. My sister failed the test, and so she was gone. I never saw her again until this evening when she knocked at my door.

"Is it too hot? Would you like something to eat?

As her stare shifted from the hot chocolate to me, I saw that look in her eyes. That same look she had as a little girl when she experienced something new, something strange. That look of wonder and excitement. I never did understand that look and never experienced it myself.

"No thanks, this is fine."

"Where are you headed to? Why did you leave the facility? Were you discharged?" I had so many questions

"I just had to leave. I couldn't take it anymore. I ran away."

"But where will go?"

"South America. I've been told that some countries there are accepting of people like me. Welcoming them actually."

"But in this weather? How will you get there?"

"We've made arrangements, that's all I can tell you."

"But why did you come here tonight?"

"I wanted to see you again. I wanted to see if you might come with me."

"But the authorities." I stuttered. "They will be angry."

"Screw the authorities," she shouted back. "It's our lives."

Yes, it is our lives I thought, but the authorities knew better. At least, that's what they told us. Those who pass can stay, those who fail will need to be removed from society until they are reprogramed. It was now the law.

"Are you sure those countries will take you in?" I asked. "After all you ..."

"Failed the test. Yes, I failed, but for them it's no big deal. And like I said, they are welcoming us to come. They actually want people like me."

"But why would they?" I had an expression of doubt as I looked at her. "Why in the world would they."

She didn't answer. Perhaps she didn't want to tell me. But she had that strange look in her eyes.

"The van will be here at sunup. You can join us if you'd like."

"But I passed the exam, I can stay here. Why would I want to go to South America? I'm happy here."

Again, she was silent. But her eyes weren't. That look again. I felt she wanted to tell me something but couldn't, or wouldn't.

"Have you seen mom and dad recently?" She changed the subject. That look was no longer in her eyes.

"Oh, I guess you wouldn't know. Why should you?"

"What?"

"The authorities are now testing people when they turn 60."

"And?"

225

"Mom passed, but dad failed. So, the authorities moved him to a facility, but we don't know where. We are hoping he can be reprogramed and that they will let him come home."

We both sat there in silence. She reached across the table and held out her hands. I did the same. We held hands. Her hands were warm now. So warm.

"It's not fair," she said.

"What?"

"These tests."

"But the authorities say they are important. That they create harmony in our society."

She just looked at me. Then she shook her head.

"But why do they get to decide?"

"Because they are the authorities. And they know best."

"And what the hell are they testing? What are they looking for?" She released my hands and jumped up. She was mad. I could see that in her eyes. Definitely angry.

"It's all in the number, you know that." I meekly replied, hoping she would calm down.

"Oh yes, the number. It's all in the number. The damn number."

"That's what they tell us."

"And just what does this number measure? They never told us."

I had no answer, I never did.

It was dawn now. The van pulled up to the curb. The headlights flashed.

"They're here," she said. "Please come with me."

"I don't think I should, after all I passed, and I can stay here where I'm comfortable."

"But damn it, you're my brother and I want you to come with me."

"You go sis, maybe you'll be happy there."

I could tell she wanted me to go, but she got up and started walking to the front door. Then she saw the results hanging on the wall.

"You framed it?" She asked. "You framed the results of your test?"

"Well of course I did. The authorities said we should. That everyone who passed should be proud and display their results."

I was standing by the framed test result. Smiling. Proud.

"Look, the results. 90. A score of 90. I passed with distinction."

"That's strange, I never got my results. They just said I failed."

"I guess they didn't want to embarrass you with your number. The authorities were thinking of your feelings. They are so thoughtful that way."

"Yes, perhaps that was it."

She moved closer to the award.

You know, I've never seen one of these before."

She was now only inches away from it. Squinting to bring the small print into focus.

"I wonder what this means?"

"What?"

"These initials right after your score."

"I don't know, never really looked that closely."

She removed the framed award from the wall and held it in her hands.

"Well, what are they?" I asked.

"Here, look here, the small letters right after your score."

"Those?"

"Yes those, those two letters, I wonder what they mean?"

"I don't know."

She put the frame back on the wall and turned to me.

"IQ, I wonder, what do they mean?"

As the van pulled away, I looked back at the framed award. IQ, that's strange. The authorities never told us what that meant. All they said was if the number was too high, you failed. And, of course, they also reminded us that they were the authorities, and they knew best.

Jimmy Conner T2000

He was holding it above his head. Waving it, for all of us to see.

"This, make sure your parents buy you one of these. We do not supply them."

Some guys were giggling. Others shaking their heads in agreement. I didn't know what to think.

He continued, "and this is important. If you don't have one, you can't play. Those are the rules."

He tossed the box to the kid in the front row.

"And make sure it's this brand. This is the best."

The box was slowly making its way around the group. Some continued to giggle.

"Hey, listen up, this is not funny. If you don't use one of these, you can really get hurt."

The box was getting closer.

"Any questions?"

My best friend was handing me the empty box. As he did, he raised his hand. I guess he had a question, but I didn't hear what he asked.

I was staring at the box. I turned it so I could read the description. Duke Athletic Supporter.

I read on. Soft open knit pouch for extra comfort and support. Breathable. Shrink proof. Maintains shape after repeated washings.

"And for God's sake, make sure you get the right size jock strap."

Now everyone around me was laughing. I was too.

"First practice tomorrow after school. Dress up and be on the field by 4. And dress up means wearing your jock." He was waving the athletic supporter above his head.

A week ago, I had tried out for the high school basketball team. Less than two hours into the tryout the coach called me over.

"Son, what's your name?"

"Michael, coach, it's Michael."

I thought he had pulled me aside to complement me on my basketball skills.

He put his hands on my shoulder and looked directly at me.

"Well Michael, I would suggest you find another sport. And that goes for your friend over there too."

I glanced over at Stew. He had just been whistled for double dribbling, or perhaps it was triple dribbling. Not sure what, but clearly it was not a good basketball move on his part.

"Jesus, what are we going do now?" I asked.

I could tell he wasn't discouraged. He never was. The optimist, I called him.

"Football. We'll sign up for football. Nobody ever gets cut from the high school football team."

Well, he was right about that. No one ever got cut. But not because everyone was so good, but because they hardly had enough guys to field a team each fall. Basketball. That's where all the guys wanted to play.

"I don't know Stew. That's a rough sport. Why don't we try out for tennis?"

"Tennis," he replied, "nobody cares about tennis. Certainly, the girls aren't interested in tennis players. And besides I don't even have a tennis racket. Do you?"

I didn't want to tell him that I got one for my birthday. The Jimmy Conner T2000. And I certainly didn't want to tell him I hadn't even opened the box yet.

A chromium plated steel racquet, just like the one Jimmy Conner uses, my parents said as I removed the wrapping paper.

"Open the box, Michael," they said.

I didn't, but simply turned the box over and over, looking at the picture of a smiling Jimmy Conner.

"Aren't you going to open the box, Michael?"

"Later, I'm meeting Stew now."

Stew was his usual talkative self. "Are you going anywhere for the summer? I see where the city pool opened. I'm thinking of applying for a lifeguard position. Did you pass that math class? My dad's thinking of going to Mexico for a while. Do you think your sister likes me?"

On and on. I just listened. And then, "did you get that basketball for your birthday?"

I just shook my head no.

"Too bad. Well, maybe next time."

Yes, always optimistic. Stew, that was him. Maybe next time.

The first day of football practice was brutal. All we did was run around the field. Running, running, running, with an occasional series of pushups and sit-ups.

A whole week of running, push-ups and sit-ups followed. Some of us wondered if we'd ever get to see or touch an actual football.

But then we did. One day the coach pulled out a large bag of old footballs.

"Today's the day gentlemen. We get to play football."

We all cheered. Our coach just smiled.

Positions. That was the next. Tryouts for various positions. Sometimes not even a tryout.

"Hey big guy, you're going to be a tackle."

But most of the time the coach would make his decision after we had run, or caught, or kicked, or had thrown the football.

By the end of the day, Stew was a running back and I was a quarterback.

Weeks and weeks of practice. Running plays. Occasionally playing defense. We may need you there if someone gets hurt. It was sure to happen.

Every afternoon I would slowly walk home, like a wounded soldier, with a different body part hurting after each practice.

"It's not broken, just a sprain. He'll be fine for the big game." The team doctor assured my parents. "He'll be fine."

Despite my bruises and occasional trips to the team doctor's office, my confidence grew. And I liked being quarterback.

Practices were becoming more intense now, but that was okay. We were becoming a team. A real football team. We all thought we were a good team too. State high school champs someone said.

The opening game was just a week away. On our home field. The school was buzzing with excitement. I told Stew it was because the basketball season didn't open for another month. "Nonsense," he said, "it's because we're so good and they all know we're going to win the State."

Yes, that optimism. Where did he get that?

Finally, the day arrived. It was a night game. The stands were full of students and parents. Cheerleaders were performing. The band too.

We were dressing in the locker room.

"Gentlemen, did you all remember your jock straps?" Coach was laughing. We joined him.

Out to the field. The stadium lights cast our long shadows across the grass. The crowd cheered as the band played the school fight song. We were ready. I looked to the stands. My parents were waving. I waved back.

This is my time I thought. I was ready for the big stage, the big game. The hell with basketball.

"Michael, come here," the coach was calling me.

"Get out there for the flip of the coin. You're the captain. Take Stew with you."

Captain, man did that sound good. Number 7, the captain.

Stew and I walked together out to midfield. We pounded each other's shoulders.

The opposing team's co-captains were waiting. So were the referees.

"Jesus, they're big," Stew said.

"What?"

"Look at those guys. They're enormous."

Yes, they were, I thought, really big. I wanted to ask him where his optimism had gone, but decided not to.

"Heads," the head official shouted. They won the coin toss.

"We'll kick off," their quarterback said. He was laughing. A kind of menacing laugh.

We shook hands. I thought he was going to squeeze my fingers into pulp. I squeezed back as hard as I could. He just smiled. A menacing smile to go with the earlier laugh.

Their kickoff went through the uprights.

"Jesus, did you see that?" Stew shouted. Any optimism was long gone.

We trotted out to the field and into our first real huddle of the season.

"Okay guys let's get this done. Let's show these guys what we're made of," I was almost screaming to overcome the noise of the crowd.

"What's the play, captain?"

Captain, oh how I liked the sound of that. Yes, you're the captain. They're waiting for you. Better set a good example and do it right now.

"Quarterback keeper, to the outside, on three."

Yes, I would set the tone. Perhaps score a touchdown on the first play. That would do the trick. Perfect.

"Hut, hut, hut." The ball hit my hands. I turned and faked a handoff to Stew. My back was to the line. Then I saw that look in his eyes. That surprised look. That oh my God look.

It was like a freight train hit me from behind. Actually, three freight trains. I saw the ball leave my hands as I fell to the grass. Everything went dark. The cheering stopped. So did the band.

I opened my eyes as the aroma of the smelling salt entered my nose.

"This should wake him up." It was the team doctor speaking.

"Michael, are you okay? Can you hear me, can you see me?"

My teammates were standing over me, my parents too.

The stadium lights were shinning in my eyes. I had a bloody nose and a headache. My back was numb from the pain.

"Michael, say something?" It was my mother.

I tried to sit up. I couldn't.

"Mom," I finally got out one word.

233

"Michael."

"Sorry, mom. Sorry, dad."

My dad jumped in, "sorry for what?"

"Sorry I didn't open it."

"What?"

"The Jimmy Conner T2000. The box."

The season ended as it started. We lost every game. I broke three ribs mid-season. Stew broke his ankle.

As we turned in our gear at the end of the season, the coach said, hope to see you next season.

"Sure coach," I said, "sure."

Walking into my bedroom that afternoon, I reached in the closet and pulled out the unopened box. As I tore away the cardboard, Jimmy continued to smile at me. Finally holding the chromium plated steel T2000 racquet in my hand, I said out loud. "Sorry coach. Next season I'm trying out for tennis."

Buenos Dias

"Buenos dias."

"Oh yes, good morning, Miguel"

"No, no, señor buenos dias, it's buenos dias."

"Aha, si, buenos dias," I replied.

"Qué te gustaría?"

"Eh?"

"What would you like, señor?"

"Beer, err, cerveza."

"Muy bueno, una cerveza."

I had been in Mexico about a week. Hadn't accomplished much. Learned three new words in Spanish. Buenos, dias and cerveza. And lost 10 pounds my first four days thanks to the diarrhea from those three street tacos I had upon my arrival. Don't drink the water they told me, but no one said anything about the street tacos.

"How are you feeling this morning?" Miguel was done with the Spanish. He could see I was too.

"Better, I'm getting better, thanks."

Well, my stomach was better, but the rest of me had a long way to go.

"Are you going to the beach today? Perhaps you'll meet some muchachas, you know, girls."

"Nah, not today."

"Well then, perhaps you should go see the cliff divers."

"Yes, perhaps I will."

Acapulco's cliff divers. A must-see tourist attraction. For 85 years, the Acapulco cliff drivers have been entertaining tourists with their dangerous plunges into the Pacific Ocean.

The first time I was in Acapulco, in my early 20s, after a night partying on the beach, I went to the tall cliff wall overlooking the Pacific Ocean not knowing what to expect. One of the divers motioned to me to climb down to a rock platform opposite the cliff wall so I could view his dive from below. As I stood on the small outcropping of rocks, the ocean splashed at my feet.

Without the assistance of ropes, the barefoot diver then climbed the sheer cliff wall in front of me, 120 feet above the crashing waves, pausing at a small shrine to the Virgin of Guadalupe for a quick blessing.

Standing on the top of the cliff, the diver calculated the right moment to dive. Watching the waves surge in and out of the small gulch which separated the cliff from where I was standing and knowing he had only three seconds in the air before hitting the water, he needed to time his jump to catch the crest of an incoming wave.

And then he dove. At first, he seemed to hang motionless like a large bird in the air above me, but then his body accelerated downward ever so gracefully, hands extended towards the water, eventually knifing into the peak of the incoming wave. It was a perfect dive.

Within seconds, he popped to the surface and swam the short distance to the rocks where I was standing. Smiling, almost laughing, he pulled himself up and stood next to me. The water from the Pacific Ocean gently sprayed us as we shook hands. A tattoo of a cliff diver glistened on his right arm. Then he dove back into the ocean as I climbed back up to the regular viewing area above.

To this day, I have no explanation for why he selected me to climb down to the crashing waves to watch his dive. I only know that was a special day for me.

It was twenty years since I first saw that magnificent cliff diver. That cliff diver who was responsible the most important three seconds of my life. Three seconds which revealed to me the true meaning of living life to the fullest.

And for a while I did. I really did. But then I got caught up in living my daily routine. Staying at my job for security, not because I enjoyed it. Hanging on to acquaintances because it was convenient, not because it was fulfilling. Going the same place for my holiday because it was comfortable, not because it was exciting.

I hadn't married. Things always got in the way. Usually, resistance to change.

So now, as I entered midlife, I had returned to Mexico, to Acapulco, in search of that feeling. That way of life the cliff diver revealed to me during that three second dive. And thus far, all I had done was lose ten pounds.

I read that midlife is a stressful time for many. Struggling with aging and mortality. But that was not the case for me. I was struggling to break free of routine. To once again live life to the fullest.

Alcohol was not the answer. Neither was medication. The self-help weekend course I took left me in greater despair about my dilemma. I couldn't shake the routine, the rut I was in. Sinking deeper with each passing day.

Acapulco hadn't changed much in twenty years. A high energy beach town made famous by the rich jetsetters in the 50s and 60s. Some were still here, but now retired in the high rises overlooking the Pacific. And they had been replaced by social influencers, the jetsetters of the 2000s.

And while the resort city had added new attractions, like the longest over the ocean zip line, the iconic ocean cove, where the La Quebrada cliff divers performed every day and night was still the main attraction. And for me, the draw to my return to Mexico. My search to regain my lost zest for life.

Wearing old leather sandals, a Dallas Cowboys t-shirt, and my bathing suit, I left my hotel. The walk to the famous cliffs was a short one. My spirits started lifting.

The visitors' viewing area was not very crowded. Some of the divers were just hanging out waiting for their turn. I was looking for him, but I didn't see him. Perhaps he's retired, perhaps he's …

I just stood there, looking confused, looking lost.

"Can I help you, señor?" I turned to see a young diver.

"Oh, I was just looking for a cliff diver I met twenty years ago. Not even sure he's still diving."

"Well, we do have some older divers here, so perhaps he is. Do you know his name?"

"Unfortunately, I don't."

"Entonces eso sera dificil."

"Excuse me."

"Without a name, that will be very difficult."

"Si, I assume so. But there is one thing."

"What is that señor?"

"A tattoo."

"Oh."

"Yes, a tattoo of a cliff diver on his right arm."

"Oh, Jose. Yes, I know him."

"Is he here? Does he still dive?"

"Si. Follow me."

And there he was. Sitting on a broken beach chair, in the shade of a large tree, was Jose. Older now, but definitely him.

"Jose, this guy was asking for you."

Looking up, Jose smiled.

I glanced at the faded tattoo.

"You probably don't remember me." I said.

"Of course I do."

He's just being polite, I thought. After all these years, how could that be possible?

Jose stood up and grabbed me by the hand. Slowly he walked me over to the viewing area. When we got to the edge, he pointed down to the small outcropping of rock near the pounding waves.

"Down there. I took you down there. Many years ago."

Jesus, how did he remember?

"I've been waiting for you to return," he continued. "I knew you'd come back."

"Waiting?"

"Yes, I could see in your eyes, that someday you would need to return. That my dive would pull you back."

Yes, that was it, I thought. I needed to recapture those three seconds. I needed to live in the moment. I needed to learn again how to live life to the fullest.

"Is it too late for me?"

"No, señor, it is not too late."

We walked out of the viewing area, along the top of the sheer cliffs. The ocean breeze was so cool, so refreshing, so comforting. The waves moved in and out of the small gulch below.

Soon we were at the edge of the cliff, looking down beyond the shrine to the Virgin of Guadalupe to the crashing waves below.

"Are you ready?" Jose asked.

"What?"

"To dive with me. To live life to its fullest. That's why you've come back? Isn't it?"

"Yes, but to watch you like I did twenty years ago."

"No señor, that will not be enough this time. This time you need to experience the dive."

"Jesus, no way. I'll kill myself."

"So, what if you do?"

So what if I do, thought? I had no good response.

Kicking off my sandals and discarding my Dallas Cowboys t-shirt, I nodded, yes.

"Just stay next to me, and dive when I say go."

My pulse was racing, my focus sharpened, I was ready.

"Go."

Suddenly I felt suspended like that large bird twenty years ago. I hung in the air. Then falling straight down to the wave below. I felt alive. I was in the moment.

I waited to enter the cold Pacific Ocean. It would happen in three seconds.

The Lord of the Elephants

We were skipping along the tops of the clouds now. White fluffy clouds. Occasionally, a break would reveal the land below.

We took a flight from Johannesburg Airport after missing our scheduled flight. Sitting in the waiting area, none of us heard the page for Palmer. They were looking for us to board, while we were waiting for the gate to open. We were at the wrong gate.

"No problem," they said as they simply booked us on a later flight. When the time arrived, they took us to the appropriate gate.

The jet engines on our African Air turbo prop hummed after we reached our cruising altitude. There was just an occasional bump on our way to Kruger National Park.

Kruger National Park, the largest and oldest national park in South Africa. A massive wilderness area linking a national park in Mozambique with a park in Zimbabwe. Kruger National Park, home to an amazing volume and diversity of wildlife.

"I can't believe you were able to book this!" she said over and over.

I was surprised too. Phone calls from Boulder, Colorado to Johannesburg, South Africa, at first seemed daunting. What time should

I be calling? What type of safari do we want? Can our not quite 16-year-old son join us? Do we need special vaccinations?

Somehow, it all worked out. And here we were the three of us on our way to a five-day safari in the heart of Africa.

Landing at a remote airport on the outskirts of Kruger, we were met by a driver from the Lion Sands Resort. The 30-minute ride in an open 4x4 Range Rover gave us our first view of what we might expect during our stay. Monkeys swinging from trees. A diversity of colorful birds. And in the distance, two large giraffes.

We arrived at Lion Sands and were greeted by a hostess carrying a variety of cold fruit drinks. We checked in and were shown to our bungalow. It was spacious and elegant. The usual furniture, plus a large king size bed fully enclosed with mosquito netting. And the best of all, a private outdoor shower in addition to an indoor bathroom. It was perfect.

The main building at Lion Sands overlooked the Sabine River, one of the most biologically diverse rivers in South Africa. Look for water buffalo and hippopotamus, we were told. And perhaps an elephant or two. Usually in the early morning. That's when they come to the river.

Early the next morning, we were off on our first real safari in our Land Rover. Our driver, Jabari, and our spotter, Mosi, were both natives of this area. Jabari navigated the dirt roads while Mosi was on the lookout for animals. Mosi also had a big rifle, that sat across his lap, which he said was ready just in case.

The dirt road was bumpy and dusty. It hadn't rained in weeks, so the dust was extra fine. It rose in the air behind us. The bush to either side of us was thick and tall. The going was slow, but we didn't care. It was perfect.

That the morning we saw elephants, a herd of zebra, and a sleeping lion. By noon, the sun was bearing down on us, so Jabari decided to park our vehicle under a large tree. The shade hardly made a difference, but it was Africa after all.

"A perfect place for lunch," Mosi exclaimed, as he jumped to the ground and walked to the back where the food and drink had been stored before we left. Strange, I thought, he left his rifle on the passenger seat.

Jabari helped us down from the elevated seats we had occupied. The view from those seats was unobstructed, but we needed help in getting to the ground.

Mosi had set up a small table a few yards from the Range Rover. Sandwiches and drinks, coffee, fruit drinks, beer and wine, our lunch for the day. We all stood around the table, enjoying our lunch and the view of the Sabine River which ran parallel to the dirt road. The river was extra wide at this spot, its dark water hardly flowing. Just perfect, I thought. I couldn't imagine a more perfect place.

Suddenly I heard it. A loud trumpeting. So did everyone else. Trumpeting, louder, and louder.

Jabari cried out, "everyone, quick to the Range Rover."

Before we could even move, they appeared. They were between us and our vehicle. Trumpeting, roaring now. Elephants. Two huge elephants.

"Up in the trees everyone, climb as fast and as high as you can. Go now."

We ran for the trees. Would they be tall enough? Strong enough?

The elephants came after us. Kicking dust and swinging their large trunks in the air. Trumpeting and roaring as they came for us.

I made it to the first tree and started climbing. The rest of the group found a bigger tree farther away and quickly started climbing.

We were all in the trees, all five of us, looking down at the elephants.

Then I heard Jabari speaking to Mosi. He was angry. "How many times do I have to tell you. Always keep your rifle with you."

Mosi said nothing. He knew he had made the one mistake spotters should never make. A potentially fatal mistake.

Suddenly the two elephants started shaking the tree I was in. Jesus, what did they tell us at the orientation meeting last night? Elephants will shake trees until their victims fall out. Happens every year when some villager climbs a tree trying to escape from an elephant. The elephant never gives up shaking until the villager falls from the tree. It might take hours, but the elephant won't stop until he has caught his victim.

And I was the victim.

With their massive trunks wrapped around the tree, the two elephants swung back and forth. The tree whipped from side to side as if it were in a fierce storm. I was getting dizzy.

"Hold on. Hold on dad." I heard their screams over and over again, as they were carried to me on the afternoon breeze, imploring me to hold on. "Hold on, hold on."

An hour maybe more of violent swinging, my arms grew tired, my hands grew numb.

Suddenly, I lost my grip on the branch, on my sanctuary branch at the top of the tree.

Falling, falling, hitting branches as I fell. Trying to grab on to the branches but couldn't. They struck me like a whip as I fell. I was falling too fast to grab on.

I hit the ground and lost consciousness.

I was groggy, but I could make out the conversation.

"He's got a very bad infection from the elephant attack. The tusks left deep wounds." He spoke with a British accent.

"What can be done, Doctor? Anything?"

"We have him on the strongest antibiotic medication we have. But we have never seen this infection before. At this point, there is nothing else we can do. We must just wait to see how he responds. I'm sorry."

"Thank you, Doctor Smith. Thank you."

The door to my room closed. She was sitting on the bed.

I opened my eyes and tried to speak.

"Hello." I was able to say hello. At least I thought so.

She didn't respond. I guess I hadn't said anything.

"Jesus, why did we have to go on this damn safari?" She was talking to herself. "Why didn't we just go to London, to the theater, like we originally planned. Why did I keep pushing for this safari?"

I wanted to tell her it was okay. I wanted to go on the safari too. But I couldn't get the words out. I couldn't speak.

The door opened.

"Hello, I'm Doctor Davies." There was a tone of despair in his voice. Another Brit I thought.

"I'm afraid the latest blood results just came back, and they don't look good."

She reached for my hand; she was trembling. "What do they show?"

"The infection is not responding to the medication. In fact, the infection is getting worse, spreading fast."

"Outlook, what is the outlook?"

"We don't think he'll make it through the night. I'm sorry. We'd also like to isolate him, since we've never dealt with an infection like this before."

"Can I have a few minutes before you do?"

"Of course, but don't stay too long. The infection could be a problem for anyone around him."

She was looking right at me. Why couldn't I speak. Then I realized I was paralyzed. I couldn't even move.

The isolation room was cold. Machines surrounded me. Lights were flashing. I was alone.

Suddenly the door opened. A doctor was standing there. He closed the door and walked up to my bed. He had a look of compassion the likes of which I had never seen before.

He reached down and touched my forehead. His hand was rough, but I didn't mind. I was happy to have someone in the room with me.

Then he spoke. "I'm so sorry for what has happened to you."

I couldn't respond, but I could move my eyes. He was old, very old for a doctor I thought. And he was hunched over, from his waist down. Arthritis, I thought. I saw his name tag, Dr. Oba Tembo. Must be an African doctor, I thought.

Tembo. I had heard that name before, but where? I couldn't remember.

He spoke again. I focused on his voice. It was raspy. Almost scratchy. Must be age, I thought.

"This should not have happened to you. I don't know why they did it."

What was he talking about? I was confused. Was I dreaming? Was I delirious? Perhaps the end was near?

"They will be punished for this. I promise."

His hands moved over my face. They were so rough, so dry. It was hard to breathe. What is he doing, I wondered? I wanted to scream out, but, of course, I couldn't.

Then he spoke in a language I couldn't understand. Some African language, I thought.

I was falling asleep. I didn't want to, but I couldn't stop myself.

The door opened. It was Doctor Smith and Doctor Davies. They move cautiously towards the bed.

"I don't understand it. He should have died last night."

"I can't explain it either."

Just then my wife rushed into the room. "Is it true? Is he okay?"

"Better than okay. It's like he was never sick. The infection is completely gone."

I pushed myself up in a sitting position. I was no longer paralyzed. As I did the three of them turned in my direction. I spoke. "Where is he?"

"Who?"

"The other Doctor, Doctor Oba Tembo. I must speak with him."

The two doctors looked at one another then back to me. "There's no one here by that name."

"Yes, Doctor Oba Tembo. He came into my room last night."

"Are you sure?"

"Absolutely, I'm sure. He was here."

"But there's no one by that name in this hospital."

Suddenly a nurse burst into the room.

"Can we help you, Zuri?"

"Doctors you have to see this. I just looked at the video of this room last night. Look at the monitor."

The monitor on the wall flicked on. There was me, in bed. Then a figure walked into the room. It was too dark to make it out. It moved close to the bed."

"What was that name again?"

"Doctor Oba Tembo"

The nurse let out a loud gasp. "Did you say Oba Tembo?"

"Yes, why, Zuri?"

"Because in Swahili, that translates to Lord of the Elephants."

We all turned back to the monitor when we heard the sound.

Trumpeting, trumpeting, trumpeting. The sound was so clear.

The figure on the monitor was now clearer. I could make out its wrinkled skin, large legs, and most of all, his giant trunk caressing my head. Oba Tembo. Lord of the Elephants, there he was.

U-Turns and Curry Rice

"This curry rice has to be the best in all of Japan."

Chika and Miyuki smiled and nodded in agreement.

"The flavor and aroma are perfect. Not too strong, but not too weak. How do you say delicious in Japanese?"

Looking up from his lunch, Chika replied, "oishii."

"Yes, yes, so oishii, so delicious."

It was our weekly lunch in Osaka. Chika and Miyuki were our best friends in Japan. Like Chika, I was teaching at a university in Osaka. He was a permanent faculty member, and I was visiting for a year.

On this Sunday, we decided to drive to the restaurant. Miyuki drove. As we passed the restaurant, I told Miyuki she would have to make a U-turn. "Not here," she replied. Surprised that she passed the intersection, I asked, "why not back there?"

She smiled and said, "another cultural difference between us and you."

"Oh, that." I laughed.

Miyuki had once told me that the Japanese will not do something unless it is specifically allowed, while in America, I had told her we do things unless we are told not to. So, she was looking for an intersection where a sign allowed for U-turns.

"The okonomiyaki is good too." Charmaine had ordered the unique Japanese pancake. Chopped cabbage, with slices of pork. Cooked right at our table. Normally, I would have ordered that, but the curry rice was so inviting.

"I'm sure it is, but today it's kare raisu."

"Nice pronunciation, Michael." Chika had been teaching me various Japanese words. Last week it was kare raisu, curry rice.

Imported from India, with a stopover in England, curry rice is one of the most popular dishes in Japan. Of course, the Japanese tweaked it to their taste, so their version is not as spicy as elsewhere. Japan's curry is sweeter, milder and much thicker.

"Oishii, oishii," I said as I continued eating. The combination of potatoes, carrots, beef and that sweet curry danced in my mouth. And the rice, cooked to perfection as it always is in Japan.

In Japan, the rice in the kare raisu plate, is set to the side. That way, one can mix the curry sauce into the rice as preferred. I liked to smother my rice with the sauce. I argued that it was easier to pick up with my chopsticks, but really, I just loved that sweet thick sauce. Charmaine would say that I like my food swimming in gravy. Today, was no exception.

Sadly, I was coming to the end of my kare raisu. The rice was gone, but some curry remained. Quite a bit, actually.

Calling over to our waiter with the customary 'excuse me', I said, "sumimasen."

"Perfect pronunciation, Michael. Couldn't be better," Chika smiled. I did too.

Looking up at our waiter while pointing to my plate of riceless kare raisu, I said, "could I please have some more rice?"

The waiter looked at me and then I heard it. That soft sucking sound as air was inhaled through his slightly opened lips. I know that sound, I thought, and it's not good. It's a prelude to someone about so say "I'm sorry, but ..."

Looking almost apologetic, the waiter said in a very soft voice, "not possible."

"Excuse me?" was all I could say.

The waiter could tell I was confused. He shook his head, and repeated "not possible."

"But I just need a little rice to finish my curry rice."

The waiter waved to the manager to come to our table. Bring in the main guy, I thought to myself. This should work.

"Excuse me, but I would like a little more rice for my kare raisu. As you can see, I have none."

"Not possible." He said. "Not possible," he repeated.

"What? Why?"

Clearly frustrated, I turned to Chika and Miyuki. "Can you tell him I just want a little more rice. Obviously, I'll pay for it."

All Japanese now between Chika, Miyuka and the manager. I had no idea what was being said. But I could tell the manager was apologizing. Perhaps they're out of rice, I thought. Perhaps he thought I wanted it without paying.

The manager and waiter left. Chika and Miyuki were smiling. I could tell they were trying not to laugh.

"What's going on? What did he say?"

Laughing now, Chika responded. "He said you couldn't order it."

"But why?"

"It's similar to making a U-turn," Miyuki replied.

"What?"

"They can't offer you a side of rice, because it's not on the menu."

That's Life

Life is good, and then it isn't.

Strange how that happens.

One day you're on cloud nine, and the next you're face down, struggling to get back up.

And it's raining. A downpour.

And, of course, you don't have an umbrella.

Strange how that happens.

It's like life doesn't want you to be too comfortable, or maybe it's playing a game with you.

Or perhaps that's just life.

"Something troublesome," the young doctor said after removing his hands from my neck. "We should have that checked out."

"What is it?" I said in a panicked voice.

"Don't know. That's why we need to check it out. I'll write a referral."

I didn't hear much of what he said after that. My thoughts kept circling back to "troublesome." Jesus, troublesome. What the hell is that all about?

So, life went from good to not so good in a split second. Troublesome, indeed.

A few months and many tests later, the troublesome turned out to be nothing.

"Sorry," was all the doctor could say.

I wanted to say, "that's life," but I simply said nothing.

I was back on cloud nine, but life had reminded me that it could, and probably would, change again, that a storm was lurking just beyond the clear horizon.

My past was full of those occasional storms.

"It may be polio."

"I'm sorry, but the hearing loss in your right ear is permanent."

But it wasn't just health issues.

"The captain is expecting severe turbulence, but rest assured these airplanes are built to withstand it."

"Your promotion has not been approved, perhaps the next time."

Of course, there were happier moments,

"Congratulations, it's a baby boy."

"Of course, I will marry you."

"Congratulations you've been promoted."

Reflecting on my life, all of the 83 years to date, I realize it's best to roll with the punches and embrace the good times.

To expect life.

Vince Lombardi, the coach of the Green Bay Packers, may have said it best when he offered the following advice,

"It's not whether you get knocked down, it's whether you get up."

Vince Lombardi's nine seasons in Green Bay were full of many successes. He won five NFL championships, including Super Bowls I and II. During the regular season he won 89 games.

He also got knocked down with 29 losses.

Clearly, he got back up.

"Be a Vince Lombardi," my dad would say. "Remember to get back up."

The Wait is Over

"Forty-six."

Her soft voice startled me.

"Forty-seven."

I was awake now.

"Forty-eight."

Rubbing my eyes, my vision cleared somewhat.

"Forty-nine."

I was in a room.

"Fifty, number fifty."

Her voice grew louder. She sounded annoyed.

"Is fifty here!"

Yes, she sounded annoyed.

"Number fifty, we don't have all day."

I turned to look behind me to see if number fifty was there.

"Fifty, please come forward, we must stick to the schedule."

Yes, she was definitely annoyed.

"We need to move on. Is fifty-one here?"

Strange I thought. That's the first time that has happened. Moving on.

"Fifty-two."

Her voice was much calmer now. Probably back on schedule I thought.

"Fifty-three."

Looking around the room, or what appeared to be a room, I realized that the walls, if I could call them walls, were ill defined. More like I was in a bubble. Or was I?

"Fifty-four."

I was getting tired again. My eyes started to close, but as they did, I heard,

"Fifty-five."

I looked down at the band around my wrist. Fifty-five in bright blue. That was my number. Finally, they called my number.

I was overcome with excitement. How long had I been waiting for my turn? It seemed like a long time, but I really couldn't tell. Perhaps it was only a few minutes.

"Fifty-five, are you ready?" It was her again.

I slowly moved to the front of the room. Although I couldn't see her, I did feel her presence. Then she spoke.

"Well, fifty-five it appears it is your turn."

"Yes," I replied.

"Are you ready, or do you want to wait?"

"Sorry?"

"You can wait if you wish. There is no penalty for skipping your turn."

"Oh?"

"Yes, it happens all the time. You would be surprised at how many decide to wait."

"Wait, really?"

"Yes, it probably has something to do with confronting the unknown."

"Unknown?"

"Yes, the uncertainty … about … about…"

"What's out there?"

"Yes, exactly, what's out there."

"Well, I'm not afraid and in fact I'm excited for it. I want to see what it's like."

"Perfect attitude. You'll do just fine, fifty-five, I'm sure."

"What do I need to do?"

"Make your way over to that dark hallway in front of you. Wait for the signal and then go through it. Simple as that."

"What signal?" I asked.

"You'll see. Just wait there," was the reply.

As I approached the hallway, I suddenly felt afraid. What was this dark hallway and where would it lead me? I started to panic as this fear washed over me.

"Excuse me, but I've changed my mind. I want to wait," I shouted.

"It's too late, the process cannot be reversed at this time. You must proceed," was the reply.

"But, I ..."

"Sorry, fifty-five it's your time."

Suddenly there was a bright light, and I was being drawn to it. I tried to resist but couldn't.

The pull got stronger and stronger.

Suddenly there were other voices.

"You're doing fine."

"He's almost here."

"Just one last ... push."

The light around me was intense, and although my vision was blurry, I could make out strange images.

Then the voices returned."

"A baby boy, congratulations."

"Oh, my goodness."

"Do you have a name for your son?"

"Yes. Henry James."

"Well, welcome to the world, Henry James."

About the Author

Michael Palmer was born in 1941 in New York City.

For 47 years, he was a finance professor at the University of Colorado in Boulder. During that time, his publications consisted solely of academic research papers.

When he retired in 2013, he continued to teach as a visiting professor in Japan, Italy and Germany.

However, when the pandemic took hold in 2020 those opportunities quickly ended.

Tired of watching tv reruns, his wife, Charmaine encouraged him to find something more exciting to pursue.

Remembering that his father published two books when he was in his 80s, Michael decided to try his hand at writing short stories. Before he realized he had written over 100.

Friends and family encouraged him to publish some of these short stories. So, in January 2023, his first book, The Last Green Flash was published. His second book, No Cappuccino in the Afternoon followed in 'June 2023.

Michael lives in Boulder, Colorado and when not writing, he and his wife enjoy traveling. His third book, Under the Marula Tree, was completed while they were spending time in Italy and Japan, and as the readier will see some of the stories in his latest book, like his two previous books, are formed from his experiences while in those counties.